I0589531

Broken

Brooke Linford

Broken
Copyright © 2017 by Brooke Linford

Cover: Indigo Forest Designs
Layout & Typeset: Close-Up Books

All rights reserved. No part of this book may be reproduced in any form by any electronic or mechanical means including photocopying, recording, or information storage and retrieval without permission in writing from the author.

ISBN-978-0-9876231-8-8

Published by Close-Up Books
Melbourne, Australia

For Ashley, with love

Chapter 1

I wanted tonight to be a success, but even as I rushed home, a dark cloud of foreboding settled over me. I'd left work early to make sure my apartment was perfect before my parents arrived. I made the bed with fresh sheets for them to sleep in, and my two fluffiest towels hung in the bathroom. I dug through the back of the pantry for the last few items Mum had given me – a rose-patterned vase and scented candles – and placed them strategically around the room. Hopefully all my preparations meant there'd be no fuel for an argument.

They showed up after an hour of me glancing frequently through the window, watching the darkening street for their Jeep. Finally, my mother swept up the stairs and stepped over the threshold.

She gazed around her, her face falling in dismay. 'Oh, Amanda, I thought you were going to upgrade this lounge suite.'

My heart sank. *Jesus, that's the first thing she says?* Ignoring the comment, I kissed her cheek, and helped Dad wheel in their suitcase.

I'd warned Giovanni and Marianne we were coming to Alberto's for dinner, and I was already dressed and ready, tapping my fingers on the bench top as my parents settled into my bedroom.

'I don't even know how you're going to get through the night on that thing,' Mum called through the bedroom curtain I'd strung between the two rooms. I heard the spray of a perfume bottle, and a moment later a heavy floral scent filled the air. 'That couch is so old. You'll wake up crippled in the morning.'

A series of snappy retorts wound through my mind, but I bit them all back. Dad sat beside me on the sagging leather couch and raised his eyebrows at me, adding a calm smile – I couldn't figure out how he managed it.

'Are you really wearing that?' Mum asked, wrinkling her nose.

She looked trim and elegant in a charcoal woollen skirt, her cardigan matching perfectly. She'd reapplied her makeup, and not a strand of her shiny hair was out of place. I surveyed my own outfit; I'd chosen it carefully, I thought. I'd tossed aside everything else, finally settling on this combination.

'What do you mean?' I asked.

'*This.*' She plucked at the sleeve of my red leather jacket with two manicured fingernails. 'Where did you get this?'

'It's Marianne's,' I murmured, feeling the familiar prickle of irritation run across my scalp.

'That girl has always had questionable fashion sense.'

Her face puckered in disgust. It was no secret my mother and my best friend couldn't stand each other. Sighing, I shrugged off the jacket and slid on a plain black cardigan instead. What was the point of arguing?

Dad flicked through a tattered magazine on the coffee table, ignoring the tension in the room.

*

Peak-hour traffic was still heavy by the time we arrived at the restaurant. I jumped off the tram and tried to walk ahead of my parents, but my mother kept me back with a barrage of criticism.

'... I'm just saying that it wouldn't hurt to look at other places to live. You don't even have a security code on the building, and your front door doesn't shut properly. Don't think I didn't notice that.'

The warm light of Alberto's spilled gently through the windows ahead. I focused on it as we neared; the sound of Mum's high heels hammering on the footpath pounded against my skull.

'And with winter coming, I can't believe you haven't spoken to your landlord about the heating. It shouldn't be up to you to buy your own electric heater. They cost a fortune to run, you know. Honestly, you need to get on to that. You're cold, and you're in a building with no security. I mean, what if someone breaks in? A rapist could walk right up to your door–'

'We're here.' I barged through the door into the crowded restaurant. The clatter washed over me – voices, cutlery scraping plates, music – and instantly I felt calmer. I released a long breath.

'You won't have to help out tonight, will you?' Mum asked as she squeezed past me.

'No, Mum, I don't work here anymore.'

'I just want to have a nice relaxing meal with my birthday girl, that's all,' she said into my ear. I almost smiled. Maybe if she stopped talking about how shit my place was then I could relax for a minute.

I found our reserved table – my regular table – and led my parents towards it. People surrounded the bar and Giovanni greeted them effortlessly as he passed by.

'*Ciao, carina*,' he cooed, scooping me into his arms. I rested my cheek against the cool silk of his shirt. 'And here they are,' he said, reaching out to my parents. 'Welcome, it has been so long since we saw you last here.'

My mother frowned, concentrating on untangling Giovanni's accent. Finally her red-painted lips curled into a hesitant smile.

'Thank you.' Dad nodded as he shook hands with Giovanni.

'Have you met Lucas yet, our new barista?' Giovanni asked me, his eyes shining.

Oh God, here we go. 'Not yet.' I kept my tone light, aware that Mum was listening hard. 'How's Luisa? Is she here tonight?'

He shook his head. '*Stanca*.' He glanced up at my parents and held his hands in front of his belly.

'Oh,' my mother sighed. 'Your wife is pregnant?'

'*Si*, our second baby. Due in four weeks.'

Mum's face lit up, and she looked at me with a smile. *Tick tock*, I could almost hear her say.

'Is Marianne in the kitchen?' I asked.

'*Si*,' Giovanni replied. 'Go, go.' He flicked his hand, slipping into my chair as I stood.

Marianne ladled sauce over a steaming mound of pasta. Her whites were stained red, her hair pulled back tight, and she wore a mask of determination. 'Helena!' she barked as I leaned against the bench, watching her work.

I missed the hustle of the restaurant, the smell of beer under my fingernails, the music and drinks at the end of the night while we slopped water across the floors. Working as a receptionist just wasn't the same.

I should have left the kitchen and rescued my parents from Giovanni's small talk, but I'd promised Marianne I'd let her know when we arrived. She wanted to be prepared for my mother – who she hated like poison – and she was desperate for me to meet Lucas, the barista. She'd been raving about him for weeks.

She kissed my forehead. 'You're here. How's it going?' She pushed her damp hair behind her ears. I knew what *it* meant.

'She's been her usual self.' I forced a smile. 'You know, my place lacks security, the heating thing ... and apparently I'm under threat of a rapist breaking through my door.'

'Christ,' Marianne moaned. 'You've lived alone for years. You lived alone in Italy, for fuck's sake–'

'Yeah, yeah.' I nodded, interrupting before she got carried away. 'Busy tonight, hey.'

She shrugged, surveying the kitchen. 'That reminds me, can you help me prep tomorrow arvo? We've got the Desio family coming in for dinner.'

'All of them?'

'Yeah, a birthday party.'

'That's fine.'

She slapped the bench top. 'Oh God, wait, have you met

him yet?'

'Lucas?' I took a deep breath, pushing away my irritation. 'No, not yet.'

'God, he's so perfect for you.'

I chuckled. 'The poor guy.'

'Where is he? He was just out here on a break.' She went to the kitchen door and peered through. 'Here. Quick!' She beckoned me over. 'You didn't see him at the bar?'

'I didn't, but my mum's here and Giovanni has an accent.'

She rolled her eyes. 'Well, Lucas started three weeks ago, you know. I can't believe you haven't been here for *three weeks*.' She pointed.

'I've been busy ...' I murmured. *And putting off this forced fix-up for as long as possible.*

At the end of the bar, Lucas worked in a cloud of steam behind the coffee machine. He was tall, thin, with long blond hair pulled back into a messy ponytail, his white sleeves rolled up to the elbows. Marianne had already worked her way into his life, and she'd been spoon-feeding me morsels of information ever since.

I knew he'd walked in off the street, desperate for work. I knew he was a trained barista who planned to source and roast his own beans one day; that he couldn't speak a word of Italian but loved Italian food. I knew, even though she hadn't told me, that Marianne had convinced Giovanni to hire him. I knew what her argument would have been – Giovanni's wife Luisa was about to give birth, and they needed someone to replace her, someone who could make coffee as great as Luisa. And I knew, by the sparkle in his eye earlier, that Giovanni was now on board to set the two of us up.

Marianne was convinced we would hit it off and that if I relaxed and went with it then ... what? All my troubles would disappear? She was sketchy on that last part.

I leaned back against the door jamb as Helena the waitress wobbled past with a pile of dirty plates. 'You know, I do have a life outside of this place,' I whispered to Marianne, who studied me carefully. 'So, what have you told him about me?'

Marianne grinned. 'Just do me a favour,' she whispered. 'Order yourself a coffee.'

I nudged her back into the hot kitchen. 'Shit, now you've made me nervous,' I said, louder now my voice had to compete with kitchen noise.

'Isn't he kind of stunning though?' Marianne mused.

'I have to get back out there,' I said, shaking my head. 'And you know you have to come talk to my mother.'

Marianne jabbed a finger at my chest. 'Just don't leave me alone with her.'

*

We ate *baccala*, crab risotto, and drank Prosecco and beer. Dad toasted me for my upcoming birthday and for a brief shining moment I was content in their company. It was a rare occurrence, and I knew that on some level I still wanted their approval; for them to be proud of me, treat me like an adult, and enjoy spending time with me. I would never admit that to Marianne.

Giovanni floated back and forth, joining us for a drink and charming my parents. Once Mum was tipsy enough to practice her basic Italian greetings on him, I took the opportunity to introduce myself to Lucas.

'You're Amanda,' he said, before I'd even opened my mouth. I raised my eyebrows in reply. 'Marianne pointed you out.'

'Yep, she's been wording him up,' Pete the barman called, stacking glasses into a rack beneath the bar.

'It's good to meet you, anyway,' Lucas said. The blue lights behind the bar cast him in an eerie glow that made my breath catch. Glancing towards the kitchen, I was pleased that Marianne wasn't spying at least. She was right about one thing; he was kind of stunning.

'You too.' Taking a breath, I shoved my hands into my jeans pockets. 'Apparently you make great coffee.'

He beamed. 'Well, what can I get for you?'

'A latte would be great.'

'What about your parents?' He lifted his chin in their direction and I looked over my shoulder. Mum threw her head back and cackled at something Giovanni said.

Oh God, she's pissed. 'I think they're fine.'

I made small talk with Pete and tried not to stare at Lucas while he prepared my coffee; hunching over the cup, swirling the milk into a feather pattern. He nudged the cup across the bar and waited, arms crossed, while I took a sip.

'It's very good.'

He grinned. 'You have a great blend here.'

I smiled back. Pete edged closer along the bar to watch our exchange. I cleared my throat, aware that everything I said or did was being scrutinised. It was warm in the restaurant, and I fought the instinct to fan my face. 'You like it here?'

'Yeah, everyone's been great.' He flicked a glance at Pete,

who whipped a tea towel out of his belt and started wiping down the bar. 'By the way, Marianne invited me to the barbecue for your birthday ...'

A flutter in my tummy. *Damn you, Marianne.* 'Okay, no worries.'

'Well, she's met my housemate Cam and they've hit it off, so she's asked him too.'

I forced a nonchalant smile. *I suck at this.* 'That's fine.'

An awkward silence fell between us. People waited behind me, but Pete hadn't seemed to notice them. I picked up my cup and saucer and shrugged, relief coursing through me that this first meeting was finally over.

'We'll talk more on Sunday, then,' Lucas said.

I nodded. 'Thanks for the coffee.'

*

Outside, the breeze snapped its teeth against my skin. Mum was still tipsy, and as we stepped onto the street, she collided with a man in a black trench coat. Instead of being embarrassed, she wrapped her painted fingernails around his sleeve, cooing, 'Well, hello there!'

He tore his arm free, disgust stark on his face.

'Sorry,' I murmured, trying to tug Mum away. His eyes slid over to me, and his mouth twisted into a sneer. My stomach clenched and I grabbed Mum again, making her stumble. 'Come on,' I hissed, yanking her behind me.

'That's the type of man you want to find, Amanda,' she said loudly as we turned to follow Dad. He was whistling on ahead, strolling towards the tram stop with his hands in his pockets. 'Not some boy with long hair who makes coffee for a living.'

I increased my pace. Adding alcohol to my mother's already insufferable personality was such a bad idea.

'Now he might be fun, but you need to get yourself a real man.'

'Oh, Jesus, you're drunk, Mum.'

'No really,' she cried, adding a shrill giggle. 'Did you see the suit on that guy? Now, he has money, and that's important. Security is important, you know that.'

Glancing over my shoulder, I saw the man lingering outside the door to Alberto's, watching us walk away. His stare made my stomach turn. *What's his problem?* The man stood eerily still. A muffled ringtone escaped his suit but he ignored it, simply staring after us as I hurried my mother along.

'I'm not really looking for a relationship right now,' I said, fighting a shudder.

'So you keep telling me.' The toe of her shoe scuffed the pavement, tripping her a little. I caught her shoulders, straightening her out.

'Then maybe you should start listening to me.' I nudged her ahead of me. 'Come on, Dad's waiting.'

Chapter 2

'Oh, it's absolutely freezing in here.'

The criticism of my apartment resumed as soon as I'd unlocked the door. It was almost a relief after the ride home, enduring her lengthy opinion of men and relationships as she slowly sobered with each jerk of the tram.

'Amanda, did you hear what I said? It's bloody freezing.'

I switched on the electric heater at the wall and didn't answer. After I made tea – using the fine china she'd given me for Christmas – we sat in silence, my mother huddled rather dramatically in a blanket on the sofa. I was desperate to get to bed; exhausted after only a few hours in my mother's company. The worst part? She was right about a lot of things. My apartment was old and cold, and it didn't have a security system. But it was home. I'd lived here for a couple of years and had loved every minute of it. It was small and dark, but that was all part of its charm. I loved the cosiness, and the kitchenette with the chipped brown-panelled cupboards, and stained bench tops. I loved the worn-out couch and overstuffed bookshelves that threatened to fall at any moment. I loved my espresso machine – the newest item in the whole place – that sat polished and gleaming in my kitchen.

Mum didn't listen when I told her I had no intention of moving, because she could never be happy in such a place. Her life was in a constant state of flux; always renovating, the furniture and appliances regularly upgraded and rearranged. My mother loved to live in a catalogue, as though she was living the dream. During my childhood, I never felt settled, never 'at home' anywhere. I was happy and proud I'd managed to find my home somewhere as an adult – places and people I couldn't live without. I loved my apartment, and Alberto's, and Marianne, and Giovanni. They were all home to me.

'You sure you're okay on the couch?' Dad asked, stacking our empty cups.

I nodded, and moved over to give him a hug. He was a big man, with a big heart, but not a lot to say. It bothered me that he didn't defend me, that he didn't tell Mum to stop criticising. But he loved her.

'Night night, sweetie.'

*

Marco stands on the balcony at Amalfi, overlooking the rough sea below. His hair streams back from his forehead, whipping in the wind. Above him on the road, hard sun beats down on me. It's so hot here; the sweat pours off me. But I'm safe. He doesn't know I'm watching.

The wind begins to howl, the balcony shakes against the cliff. He turns, sees me, his dark eyes frantic. He screams my name. I don't want to go to him, but my legs disobey, moving slowly, taking me to him. As I near, I taste the salty air; the wind hurls the scent at me, the mist cools the sweat on my skin. The sun has disappeared. I shiver.

I reach the stone steps that lead down to the house but now I can't move. The waves are thrashing at the rocks, spitting white froth. I'm frozen. Marco's scream cuts through the air; the balcony comes away from the side of the cliff. I watch, helpless, as everything crumbles, and Marco falls to the rough sea below.

*

I woke with a cough, gasping for air. *Marco.* I sat up in the still-dark apartment, my legs slick, sweat dampening my hair. Marco, Marco, Marco. I shouldn't still be thinking about him. I shouldn't still be dreaming of him. From my bed, my dad snored happily, the rumble echoing through the apartment. I peeled the blanket off and flexed my feet in the cool air. My back ached from the soft couch. Damn it, Mum was right.

I stood, wobbled, and stretched. The dread hadn't lifted. The dream haunted the room, but now that I was awake, Marco's face wasn't clear anymore; only a blur of the details I couldn't forget – black wavy hair, piercing dark eyes, cheeks and chin that never lost their stubble.

I rubbed my lower back, pressing in my fingers. Tonight had left me feeling queasy, but it wasn't only the dream. It was my mother. And Lucas. And the pressure from Marianne and from Mum to meet a man and settle down. The creepy man in the trench coat, a man with money and class.

Two women pulling me in different directions.

At the kitchen sink, I gripped a glass of water and

took a sip. My hand shook; my feet cold against the floor. I wasn't interested in starting a relationship. And it wasn't just Marco and my time in Italy that pushed me away from it – but everyone pressuring me into having another. Why couldn't Marianne see that? She had hand-picked Lucas for me before I'd even met him. He seemed nice, but that didn't mean he was my soul mate.

I sat at the kitchen table, curling my legs underneath me, and gulped down the rest of the water. My friends insisted I should have counselling to deal with this mistrust towards others, and maybe they were right, but somewhere below that rational, soothing voice in my ear was the dread. *The dread.* I couldn't depend on anyone but myself.

*

'Good, you're here. My wrists hurt.' Marianne shoved a vegetable peeler into my hand. In front of us on the bench was a huge mound of peeled potatoes, glistening white. Beside them, an even bigger pile, still in their grubby skins.

'No hello? I'm here out of the goodness of my heart, you know.'

'Hello, hello, hello.' She nuzzled her face into my neck. 'Now help me.'

I laughed. 'Okay, let me wash my hands first.'

'So, how was last night?' she called, as I lathered up at the sink.

I told her about my mother tripping in the street, flirting with the strange guy in the trench coat, and the extra nagging back at my apartment.

'Yeah, so you didn't sleep well. You look like shit.'

'Thanks,' I shot over my shoulder.

'Have they gone at least?' she asked, grimacing.

'Yes,' I reassured her. 'They left this morning.'

'Good,' she huffed. 'Hey, Lucas is starting soon–'

'Yeah, look,' I said as I turned to her. 'About that? Knock it off.'

She shrugged. 'What?'

'You know, the whole fix-up bullshit. I'm not interested. And you know why I look like shit? Because I had that dream again – about Amalfi and the house and the balcony.' *And Marco.* But I didn't say it; she knew which dream I meant.

She wrapped an arm around my shoulder. 'I get it, but you need to let that crap go. You know that.'

'I know.' I took a breath. 'How do I do that? It's so stupid.'

She pulled away. 'It's not. Just try and relax, okay?' She grabbed some paper towels and wrapped them around my dripping hands. 'And be nice to Lucas. You can be a real bitch to anyone who happens to have a penis. But he's really nice.'

I smiled. 'Yeah, I heard you invited him and his housemate to my barbecue.'

She grinned. 'Cam. He's a brickie.' Her voice dropped to a whisper. 'He has these hands, they're all rough and chapped and I can't help but imagine–'

'Yep, I thought so. And this is where I walk away and peel those damn potatoes.'

*

When Lucas walked into the kitchen, my fingers were red and stiff and cold. Six remaining potatoes mocked me from the bench top.

He grinned at me. 'I thought you quit.'

'So did I.'

I heard him behind me in the store room, locking away his bag. I glanced at Marianne; she was dicing tomatoes and kept her head down.

'Can I get you both a coffee?' Lucas asked, appearing beside me. He was close; folding up the sleeves of his crisp white shirt, his fingernails freshly clipped. Marianne's description of Cam's hands echoed through my mind and I looked away.

'Yeah, the usual,' Marianne replied, knife thumping the board. *Chop, chop, chop.*

'Short black.' Lucas nodded. *Chop, chop, chop.* 'Amanda?'

I made myself look up. His eyes were a pale blue, crystal clear. I managed a nod.

'Latte?' he pressed.

I reached out to stop him walking away, and when my hand brushed his forearm I pulled it back. 'Actually, I'll have a short black too.' Embarrassed, I pretended to flex my raw fingers, rubbing to warm them. *What's wrong with me?*

As he left the kitchen, pushing through the doors, I went to the sink to run hot water over my hands. Behind me, Marianne snorted. 'Not interested, my arse.'

'Damn you!' I spat.

Chuckling, she dropped the knife on the board. 'You're welcome.'

*

I ran towards the ding of the tram, my aching feet carrying me well. I jumped on, thumping down on a torn vinyl seat.

I'd avoided Lucas for the remainder of the afternoon, but it hadn't been easy. I'd been caught off guard in the kitchen and Marianne had seen it. Now she would never give up.

The tram creaked back into action and I turned to look outside. The man from last night stood on the other side of the grimy window. No trench coat this time, but it was definitely him. Dark hair, dark beard, dark eyes. My mother's *Mr Perfect*. He stared, black eyes burning into me, his lips twisted in a cold smile. I shrank back in my seat. *What the hell?*

I swivelled my face away, but I could still feel him there, eyes boring into my back. I glanced over my shoulder and there he was, walking closer, eyes wild. My heart leapt into my throat.

But he stopped, face only inches from the glass.

As the tram gathered speed, blurring his pale face with the other few pedestrians that remained at the stop, I made myself turn away. I blew out a breath, rolling my shoulders to loosen them.

I needed to relax.

Mum's drawn some freak's attention onto me; someone she thinks would be an ideal partner. Am I imagining it, or is he really staring at me with crazy eyes?

Mum never failed to confuse me, to turn my world upside down. Why did I let her do that?

*

As I approached the park, Giovanni's voice carried out into the street. 'The sausages! I said the sausages!'

I pushed through the gate and walked towards the

barbecue area. Under a huge corrugated iron shelter stood Lucas, Pete and his girlfriend, and a guy with a shaved head who must have been Cam. Off to the side, Marianne and Luisa sat with Oscar at a picnic table under the watery sun, arranging bowls of salad and paper plates. Giovanni turned from the sizzling grill and dashed over to me, an apron over his blue silk shirt. He tucked barbecue tongs under the waist cord of his apron, as if they were a sword and he was going into battle.

'Birthday girl.' He hugged me, and I inhaled his coconut hair cream. 'Everyone is here, come on.'

'Manda!' Oscar bolted towards me, throwing his entire body weight at my legs and tackling me to the ground. The dewy grass bit through my denim jeans, but I couldn't help bite my lip to hold back a laugh.

'Oscar, you shouldn't do that,' Giovanni tutted, but he was smiling.

I pulled Oscar onto my lap and tickled his belly until he shrieked with laughter. When he started to hiccup, I stopped. He sighed to catch his breath, resting his forehead against my chest. I stroked his dark curly hair until he sat up. 'You know not to mess with me, right?'

'Yep,' he giggled, wriggling out of my arms. 'Manda, I've got a present for you. I'll go get it.' Like a spring, he bounced to his feet and ran back towards his mother.

I followed him, grinning as I approached Luisa, who was pouring wine into glasses.

'My God, you're huge,' I cried, spreading my hands across her belly. 'Please tell me you've stopped working. You've stopped, right?'

'Don't worry,' Marianne murmured, collecting a glass.

'She'll keep working until the baby drops right out of her.'

Luisa smiled and then kissed both cheeks. 'I'm slowing down. I'm fine, really. I've done it all before.' She patted Oscar's head and passed me a glass of wine. 'Please tell *me* you're going to make a move on that sweet boy.' She nodded towards Lucas, who was still standing with the others but didn't seem to be paying attention to what they were talking about – he was looking at me.

'No, I'm not,' I said to Luisa. 'But I am going to say hello.'

Oscar blocked my path, holding up a shiny red parcel. 'I picked it out. But Mama wrapped it.'

'Ooh, well, let's see.' I sat on the wooden bench next to him, tearing at the paper. Inside was a knitted purple and white striped scarf. 'You picked that out? I love it.'

Oscar beamed. 'Mama said we had to get it because it's cold outside.'

'That's true. It's almost winter.'

'You don't want to catch a cold.'

I planted a kiss on his forehead. Immediately he wiped it off. 'Thank you, sweetie. Have you met our new friends Lucas and Cam?'

'Yep. They got here ages ago.'

He jumped up and ran towards them, leaving me with a lapful of torn red paper. I wrapped the scarf around my neck and sipped my wine. Marianne plopped down next to me.

'Okay, birthday girl, what's the plan?' She grabbed the end of my scarf and twirled it around her fingers.

'Why are you asking me? You planned this thing.'

She moaned. 'No, not the fucking barbecue. *Lucas.*'

I shot her a warning glare. 'What about you and Cam and his rough, manly hands?'

She smirked. 'Yeah, okay. He's a sweetheart, but I'm not going there.'

I paused, mid-sip. 'Are you kidding me? When have you ever not gone there?'

'Fine, I'm a slut. I don't know. It would be good to just be friends.'

My glass was frozen beneath my lips. 'What the hell is going on with you?' I whispered. 'No, really, mid-life crisis?'

'Fuck you, I'm not that old.'

I grinned. 'I should go say hello. Come with me.'

In the shelter, I kicked dry leaves out of the way that had blown in from outside. The concrete floor was dusty and cold; the sun hadn't been able to make its way under the roof.

Cam was stocky and shorter than Lucas. Smiling warmly, he stuck out one of those strong hands for me to shake. 'Happy birthday,' he said. His hands seemed to match the rest of him. His face was weathered but friendly, cheeks rough with stubble. Muscles bulged beneath his sleeves.

'Thanks.' I shook my hand free of the firm grip. 'It's not my birthday until Thursday. Everyone's making a fuss.'

'Well, happy birthday for Thursday.'

I smiled. 'Thanks. So, you guys live together.'

'Since high school,' Cam answered.

'I've got a present for you,' Lucas said to me, pointing to the edge of the shelter. A brown paper bag was propped on the narrow bench that ran around the edge of the corrugated iron wall.

He walked towards it and I followed. His jeans were slung low and he walked with a slight limp, putting more weight on his left foot. It was as though his right leg couldn't straighten properly – I hadn't noticed that before.

Lucas leant over and slid a flat rectangle out of the bag.

It was a painting of the Amalfi coast. Ragged rock and white-topped waves threatened the precariously-placed buildings above. My heart lurched and I sank onto the freezing seat. *Marco. Disappearing into the sea.*

'Marianne said you lived in Italy for a while. I knew I had this somewhere at home, and anyway, I found it. My mum painted it. She travelled through Italy years ago.'

I didn't know what to say. He was standing above me, looking down at the painting, waiting for me to respond. 'Your mum painted this?' I finally choked out.

'She paints, yeah. I've got a lot of her work, but I like this one. Marianne said you used to have holidays on the Amalfi coast.'

My fingers were clammy against the painting's edges. I rested it against my knees. Lucas wasn't to know the significance of the painting; Marianne wouldn't have told him everything, but the gift was a dreadful reminder of the worst time in my life. 'That's true. I loved it there. Thank you so much ... you didn't have to get me anything.'

He shrugged. 'That's okay.'

I stood, cradling the painting in the crook of an arm. He was so much taller than me. I lifted my chin to look into his eyes. His brown jacket was zipped up his chest, and at his throat was the edge of a ragged T shirt. He took a step aside so I could pass, and as he did, a flicker of pain crossed over his face. He huffed a breath and turned away.

'What's wrong?'

He glanced down at me and shook his head. 'It's nothing.'

'Is it your leg? You were limping.'

He didn't answer straight away and a dark cloud drifted

over his face. 'I broke my leg six months ago,' he answered. 'Car accident.'

I hesitated, alarmed by his expression. 'Oh ... and it still hurts?'

'It was complicated. It's still healing.'

'You should sit down.'

He forced a smile, his lips thin. 'Sit with me.'

I helped him sit. His face was set and hard – a pale mask. He stretched his right leg out in front of him, and placed a hand gingerly over his knee. I sank down beside him, brushing dust and cobwebs from the seat as I turned to face him. The day was overcast, the wood palings and concrete chilly beneath me.

'I'm all right,' he said. 'Talk to me. Distract me.'

'Okay ... But there's no point talking about myself since you work at Alberto's now. You probably know everything.'

He smiled, and the mask seemed to lift. 'Maybe.'

'Why don't we talk about you? I don't know a lot, really.'

'What do you want to know?' he asked.

I considered asking him about the car accident, but thought better of it. 'Well, what about your family? I know your mum paints.'

He nodded, and he moved his hand off his knee. 'My mum paints. And travels.'

'Is she travelling at the moment?'

'She's in Japan with my brother, Ben. He's living there for a bit.'

'Are you close?'

'Me and Ben are, yeah, when he's around. He travels a lot, too. I went with him for a bit after high school, Cam too. But I got sick of it. Besides, I like Melbourne.'

'What about your dad?'

'I never met my dad.' He sighed, relaxing a little more against the wall of the shelter. 'I had Cam's family. His dad. And Doug. He lived next door to us growing up, and he helped raise Ben and me. Mum would go away and we'd stay with him.' He shrugged; a nonchalant gesture, but his eyes had narrowed. 'We lived with Doug most of the time. He became my dad.'

'Were he and your mum ...'

'No, no. They were friends. He's older.'

I glanced down at the painting, still in my lap. My tummy flipped, but taking a deep breath, I acknowledged the skill involved – it looked exactly like the real thing. 'Your mum is amazing, this is beautiful.'

He nodded. 'Yeah, she's good.'

Silence fell between us. I glanced across the shelter at Cam, who stood chatting easily to Pete, hands gesturing. The murmur of conversation surrounded us but we were immune in our shadowy corner.

'So you like working at the doctor's clinic?'

I raised my eyebrows. 'Yeah, the hours are more stable than at Alberto's. I miss it though.'

'You seem to still come round a bit.' He smiled, and his teeth glowed white in the dim light of the shelter. His face was relaxed. He seemed to have forgotten all about the pain in his leg.

'True. It's hard to stay away.'

Chapter 3

I sat with Oscar while we ate. He kept me busy, distracted from the unease churning in my belly. I hadn't had a relationship since Marco, I hadn't even been close. I listened hard as Oscar chatted about his friends and the footy, dropping a hunk of meat on my shoe and then spilling tomato sauce on my thigh. Avoiding eye contact with Lucas throughout the meal was a weak attempt to extinguish the fire Marianne had lit.

After we'd chucked out the plates and refilled our glasses, I found a patch of dry grass and settled down with my wine. Everyone was busy talking amongst themselves, and I closed my eyes, trying to catch my breath. Part of me actually hated my birthday; the forced cheer, the get-togethers, the strained visit from my parents ... exhausting.

'Hey.' Lucas. Silhouetted against the cool afternoon sun. I couldn't see his expression, but wisps of his hair caught the light, outlining him in gold. 'Company?'

'Sure.'

He stretched out on the grass beside me. 'So, you didn't

really say what your plans are for Thursday. Are you doing anything special?'

I toyed with my glass. 'Oh, just working, probably. Might come to the restaurant for a meal, not that I don't do that all the time anyway.'

'You should do what you like, I guess.' He cleared his throat. 'Hey, do you want to go for a walk?' He was resting backwards, his palms flat behind him. He held my gaze. 'We could check out the rest of the park.' He lifted his chin. A gravel walking track wound between tall, shady trees – another place the sun didn't seem to reach.

I discarded my wine and sat up. 'You want to go for a walk?'

'Only if *you* want to.'

I could feel the weight in the words. I hoped he hadn't been pressured to ask, that he hadn't been cornered by Marianne and the fix-up crew. But his eyes were intense. He looked nervous. I took a deep breath. 'All right then.'

We left behind Cam and Giovanni kicking a miniature football with Oscar, and the others drinking at the picnic table.

'Is your leg still hurting?' I asked, but he only shrugged, following me across the grass and onto the walking track. The path was quiet except for our crunching steps. The sun wasn't visible here; trees tall and bending towards us, closing us in.

'Is that a pond up there?' Lucas asked, pointing ahead.

I slowed my steps. I'd never ventured over to this side of the park before. It was shadowy, cold. I didn't like it.

'Come on.' He kept walking between the trees, eyes ahead. I followed, passing empty park benches until we came to the pond. It wasn't pretty, but murky, dull, surrounded by tall reeds that seemed to hiss as they moved. A lone duck drifted morosely over the dark surface.

Lucas sat first. Suppressing a shiver, I sat beside him.

'You know, everyone's trying to get us together,' he said. He was staring straight ahead at the water, at the reeds rattling in the breeze.

'I know.'

He turned to me then. 'Marianne isn't exactly subtle, is she?' he chuckled.

'I've never known her to be subtle, no.' *Damn it.*

He cleared his throat. 'So, can I ask you something?'

'Sure.'

'Are you … Marianne told me about you and Marco …'

I suppressed a sigh. 'Okay.'

'She said you had a bad breakup.'

The sigh escaped. 'Yeah, it was about two years ago, though.'

He shifted, sitting up straighter. Out of the corner of my eye, a second duck waddled towards the pond. 'She said it was pretty rough.'

I forced a laugh. 'Oh God.'

'Sorry—'

'No, it's—'

'It's none of my business—'

I waved away his words. 'It's really okay. I don't know. Apparently I have trust issues.'

'Marianne says this, doesn't she.'

It wasn't a question. After only three weeks at the restaurant, he knew her pretty well. He was a fast learner.

'I've known her a long time. She's like my sister.'

'You disagree with her?'

I shook my head, my heart racing, my feet beginning to twitch in the gravel. I wanted to get up and run. Away from the shadows and into the light.

He shrugged. 'Sorry if I've made you uncomfortable ... I just ... I don't like it when people try to fix me up with someone I don't know.' He glanced across at me. 'You know what I mean?'

My heart slammed into my stomach. *Damn Marianne.* 'I'm sorry about Marianne. She's always been like that.'

'I haven't been at Alberto's for very long.'

My heart pounded at his words. I couldn't wait to get stuck into Marianne.

'She kept talking about you, and it was obvious what she was up to.' He smiled, his eyes sparkling, somehow, in this light. 'But I'm getting used to her.'

The breeze was getting stronger, shaking the reeds and the leaves, but everything felt still and heavy, as if I was slowly descending under water. My throat tightened. Without breathing, I tried to tear my gaze from his but I couldn't. I watched as his eyes settled on my lips and a bolt of heat travelled through me. How I wanted to reach out and trace my fingers over his, to feel his skin. But I couldn't. This situation had become alien, uncomfortable.

The instinct to run grew stronger, the toe of my boot scraping grooves through the gravel. But as we stood to walk back to the others, I couldn't deny the desire surging through my body.

*

No one had seen us leave, but they saw us return. A cake was on the table, decorated white with clumsy red squiggles of icing around the edges. The candles had been arranged on top, unlit. Everyone was sprawled out over the grass as if they had given up waiting. Oscar saw us first, jumping to his feet.

'About time,' he yelled, his small voice travelling across the park. Marianne threw her head back and laughed.

'Sorry, honey,' I said, as we approached. 'Lucas and I went for a walk.' Everyone was staring at me, including Lucas, but I just sat at the table, pulling Oscar into my lap. 'Okay, let's do this.'

Everyone sang Happy Birthday, and holding Oscar a safe distance from the flames, we blew out the candles together. Using serviettes as plates, we ate the packet-mix cake. Lucas sat next to me, smiling as I shoved my leftover cake into Oscar's mouth, making him giggle with cheeks bulging, and red icing coating his teeth. They all knew that something was brewing with Lucas and me – that much was obvious by the looks on their faces – but I tried to keep my distance, edging my knee away from his as he leaned over for more cake. When he casually brushed a hand over mine as I passed him a serviette, I excused myself, muttering about more wine. I wandered into the shelter, where Marianne and Luisa were packing leftover food into plastic shopping bags. Marianne was planning to stay over at my place tonight, and the thought of downplaying the situation was already exhausting. I didn't want to talk about my feelings or have to explain them. I didn't want her to make a big deal.

I pulled her aside. 'Listen to me.'

She grabbed an empty salad bowl to her chest. 'What?'

'Don't go on about Lucas anymore, okay? It's too much pressure.'

Her eyes widened. 'You like him, don't you?'

'See? Right there!' I jabbed a finger at her. *Why do I have to run everything by Marianne anyway?* 'You can't push the two of us together. It's offensive. Jesus, you're acting like my mother.'

Her mouth fell open, then hardened into a thin line. 'Take that back.'

'I will not.' Lifting my chin, I stared hard at her, even though I'd just said the one thing Marianne wouldn't want to hear. I couldn't back down; I had to make my point.

'I am *not* like your mother.'

'You're acting just like her. You might be right about Lucas, but you're pushing too hard.' I shook my head for emphasis.

'Well, now I'm scared to point out that you said I might be right.'

'Can you let me do the talking? But not now. Later. I'll talk about it later.'

'I'm still staying over, then? You're not shutting me out?'

'You can stay but remember what I said. Just give me a break.' I took a couple of steps then turned back. 'I'm serious.'

She nodded. Unlike my mother, she knew when I was pissed off.

*

Marianne and I sat cross-legged on the floor folding my washing.

'Okay, so you went to the pond, and then what?' She crunched on a wedge of apple as she smoothed a pair of pyjama pants on the carpet.

'Nothing; we talked a bit, then we walked back.' I accepted a piece of apple from the plate. 'Although, he said something about how everyone thinks we're perfect for each other–'

'Yeah?' Marianne cut in, folding a pair of my underpants.

'You've convinced him too, I think,' I finished, rolling my eyes. 'I think he wanted to come home with me.' The dryer rumbled to a stop from its place under my kitchen bench. I picked up the washing basket to fetch the new load.

'Good. But I'm a little confused that you chose me over him, I gotta say,' Marianne called.

'Too soon.'

'Yeah, you should probably consider getting some new underwear first.'

'Why? What's wrong with it?' I dumped a bunch of fresh towels on the carpet in front of her.

'It's so *ordinary*.' She emphasised the word as though nothing could be worse. 'Is this seriously what you wear all the time?' She held up a pair of grey Bonds bikini briefs.

'No, I've got others.' I took a towel from the pile.

'Show me.'

'I am *not* showing you my underwear drawer.'

'I'm just saying that if you end up in bed with Lucas, you might want to consider upgrading.'

'So, what you're really saying is that I should walk around in lingerie just in case I end up having sex?' I made a face. 'Do you really think a guy who is about to have sex is going to see a pair of underpants and go, "Um, nope, I've changed my mind"? They're just trying to take them off.'

She cackled, tossing the undies at me. 'Okay, point taken.'

'And, hang on,' I continued. 'Don't tell me you don't wear Bonds just in case you end up with someone.'

'Well,' she grinned. 'We're not talking about me anyway. What do you think is going to happen? Oh, and I'm asking in a non-pushy, non-mother way.'

I shrugged. 'I don't know.' I paused, remembering how my body had reacted sitting so close to him earlier. 'I like him though.'

She threw her hands into the air in a gesture of exaggerated joy. 'Finally! I have to say, don't ever doubt me again.' She grabbed a towel from the pile. 'I know you. And you've got to admit, Lucas is a bit more your type than your mother's Mr Perfect, hey?'

I shuddered, remembering that cold smile, that creepy stare. 'I know. Can you see me with some older rich guy who wears a suit and trench coat?'

'God, it's frightening how little she knows you.' She frowned, and picked up another piece of apple. 'Although, Marco was a suit, and older, and you picked him.'

His name speared into me and I shook my head. 'I didn't *pick* him. I was brainwashed by him. I was in Italy and alone. He gave me holidays and–'

'And he was an arsehole.'

'He made me feel important for a while.'

The painting Lucas had given me rested against the mirror in my bedroom. I didn't know where to put it. In a way, I wanted to hide it, and forget about it, but it was too beautiful. Every time I looked at it I thought of Marco, but maybe over time that would change. Marco and Lucas were polar opposites; Marianne was right. Maybe I could look at the painting one day and think of Lucas instead, and that would change my memory of the Amalfi Coast into something positive.

Maybe the dreams would finally stop.

Chapter 4

At five pm I was in the staff toilet at work, struggling into a fresh shirt and scrubbing at my damp armpits with toilet paper. I reapplied deodorant and replaced my blazer, bumping my elbows on the cubicle walls.

Karen noticed as I fished my handbag out from under the front desk. 'Where are you off to?' *Unbelievable.* Nothing got past her.

'Just having dinner at Alberto's.'

'Have fun,' she smiled. 'See you tomorrow.'

When I arrived at the restaurant, it was dark and the street empty. Quiet nights stressed Giovanni out, but it would make it easier for Lucas and me to talk. Parked cars glistened under the street lights, patiently awaiting their owners. I passed empty storefronts, darkened dress displays, the eerie glow of an ATM as I headed towards the light spilling onto the footpath from the restaurant windows. Nothing but the soft thump of my boots on the concrete, the fog of my breath. I was right out front when a car door swung open on the opposite side of the road and a man stepped out.

My footsteps faltered; it was him again. Mr Perfect. The car's interior light flicked off as he slammed the door, jolting me. But it was him. A flash of panic rippled across my skin. I was only steps away from the safety of the restaurant. It was okay. *I* was okay.

He stretched his arm outward, raising it above his head. I watched as a white glow emanated from an object in his palm. *A phone.* In the heavy silence, I heard a click, and a flash lit up the night.

He took a photo of me. He took a photo of me!

I turned and pushed through the door to Alberto's – into light, into warmth, into safety. Gentle music swelled from the speakers, the smell of garlic hung in the air. I let out a ragged breath and stood still for a moment, my heart thumping.

Was this guy following me? Three times I'd seen him now, each time near the restaurant. And who the hell stood there to take a photo of someone? I didn't know him ... I was sure of it.

I clenched my fists as anger flickered inside. Since that night my mother had batted her eyelashes at him, it was as if she had drawn his attention onto me. *Unwanted* attention. I glanced over my shoulder; from where I was standing, I couldn't see him or his car.

'Hey,' Lucas called.

'Hey, can you come outside with me for a minute?'

Not waiting for an answer, I opened the door and stepped back into the street. The man's car was still there, but he wasn't standing beside it. Either he was sitting inside or had walked away. His car matched his clothes perfectly – a black

BMW that had money and class stamped all over it.

'What's going on?' Lucas squeezed my shoulder.

I shook my head. I'd been scanning the street and completely ignoring him. I wasn't going to waste another second when I was here now, with Lucas. 'Sorry. Hi.' I smiled up at him. 'How are you?'

'I'm good,' he chuckled. 'Are you okay?'

'Yes. But I definitely need a drink.'

'Ah, I can help you with that.' He took my arm and guided me back to the door. 'Come on, it's cold out here.'

Back in the warmth, I took a seat at the bar and exhaled as Lucas poured me a beer. 'So what was that about?'

I took a sip. 'I thought I saw something. There's been–' I shook my head, deciding not to mention it. 'Nothing. It was nothing.' The restaurant was almost empty, and I couldn't see Pete anywhere. 'Are you on the bar tonight?'

Lucas nodded and blew out a breath. 'It's quiet. Giovanni said he'd do the bar if it gets busy.' Shouting broke out in the kitchen – Marianne's voice. Lucas and I exchanged a smile.

'I hear the Alberto's Nazi. She really shouldn't do that.'

Lucas raised an eyebrow. 'Is it weird I'm used to that already?' He pointed at the few diners scattered around. None of them had looked up from their meals. 'No one seems to mind.'

'Regulars.'

'Oh.'

Giovanni poked his head through the kitchen door and caught my eye. '*Carina*, I bring you a plate.'

Lucas wiped a spill from the bar. 'So, you're here by yourself tonight?'

I put down my glass; I was drinking too fast. The beer

was already blurring the edges a bit, sloshing into my empty stomach. 'Yeah, I come here by myself all the time.'

Our eyes met. It was obvious he liked me, and knowing this made me shaky. I pushed back my hair, wishing I'd worn it up instead. It was warm in here, and talking to Lucas made me feel warmer. My hair was getting too long anyway, almost halfway down my back now. I felt way too hot.

Giovanni swung through the kitchen door and hesitated in front of me. He held a steaming plate. 'Bar?'

'I'll talk to you later,' I said to Lucas.

I ate alone at my regular table; salmon with capers and crispy lemon potatoes. As I listened to Lucio Battisti and shot the occasional glance at Lucas, my breath caught. The soft yellow light in the restaurant made him look almost dream-like, and the light above the bar's mirror shone gold on his hair whenever he stood still. It was early and new customers were filing in sporadically, adding to the hum of chatter above the music. I watched him work the coffee machine, pour beer and wine. Even from the other side of the restaurant I could see his white shirt pull tight across his shoulders, the collar coming apart to reveal a triangle of skin whenever he reached for a bottle. I was so busy trying not to look in his direction that when Marianne came out for a visit, thumping down in her stained whites, I jumped.

'How's the salmon?'

'Great.'

She grinned at me. 'He knows you're watching him,' she whispered.

'What? I'm not–'

She laughed, nudging me across the table. 'I'm kidding.'

*

I left at eleven, and as the door swung shut behind me, I was met with bitter air and quiet. *Mr Perfect.* I scanned the row of cars for his shiny, black BMW. Still there. I strained my eyes, but the windows were tinted.

This was ridiculous. Taking a couple of steps forward, I perched on the gutter. *Should I check the car out?* I could walk back into the restaurant and wait for Marianne to drive me home. No, *that* was ridiculous.

The anger built again. The more I tried to rationalise it, or excuse the fact that this stranger had taken a photo of me, the more frustrated I became. I'd had such a nice night, and I was able to forget about this weird situation for a few hours. After my meal I'd helped Lucas behind the bar, and we'd talked and laughed and I actually felt relaxed. It was still a familiar post for me, pouring beers and chatting to customers, and I missed it. How could I have forgotten what awaited me outside? I didn't want to feel vulnerable and afraid when I had to go home to an empty apartment–
No.

Fuck this.

I stepped off the edge of the gutter and strode towards the car. The engine purred to life and the headlights flicked on. I tried to peer through the tinted glass at the blurred face. A man. Dark hair. Dark beard. Before I could move any closer, the car roared away up the street, the side of it almost clipping me as I staggered back onto the footpath. I caught my breath, pressing my hands against my stomach.

It was him. He'd been waiting the whole time? For me? What the hell was going on? I made it back into the restaurant's warm light, only the music had been changed to something louder, something fiercer, something that, despite the silence outside, I hadn't been able to hear.

Marianne was stacking chairs and noticed me immediately. Concern creased her sweaty face. 'What's wrong?'

'I need to talk to you out the back,' I hissed. Lucas was mopping up the bar with Giovanni and hadn't noticed me. I strode into the bang and clatter of the kitchen and we huddled by the door to the storeroom.

'What is it?' Marianne whispered.

I took a breath. 'I think someone's following me.'

*

'Okay, so this doesn't make sense.'

Marianne and I stood outside the back door to the restaurant, leaning against the cold brick wall. The narrow alley was like a long, dark tunnel. Wide enough for Marianne and Giovanni's cars and the restaurant's stinky rubbish bins, but not much else. I was so spooked, that if the clichéd black alley cat had streaked past us, I wouldn't have been surprised.

'Your mum walks past a man in a coat on Friday night after dinner, flirts a little, and then ... what? Oh, he was at the tram stop on the corner on Saturday afternoon, and in a car out the front tonight. Don't you get it?'

'What?' I snapped. I would never have mentioned it if I thought Marianne was going to mock me.

'He lives in the neighbourhood. Either that or he actually comes to this restaurant for dinner sometimes, did you think of that?'

'He was staring at me,' I protested. 'It was weird. And I

think he took a picture of me!'

'I doubt it. He was probably just looking at his phone.'

'But I heard a click, I saw a flash. It was the camera.' I'd been so certain before, but now I was starting to feel silly. Maybe he *was* just looking at his phone. Did I imagine it? No, I didn't. Something was going on. The anger rose again, burning away the doubt.

She pursed her lips. 'You know, if he lives nearby I'd probably even recognise him.'

'Well, excuse me for not pointing him out!'

Marianne sighed and gave my arm a squeeze. 'You need to relax. God, a random guy is looking at you, take it as a compliment. Maybe he came back because he thinks you're hot. Maybe it's all one giant coincidence.' She shrugged. 'Maybe you're nervous about Lucas so you're noticing all kinds of shit, who knows?'

I shook my head; not because I disagreed with her reasoning, but because she'd made me feel like an idiot. I never should have said anything. 'Forget it.'

She loosened her hair from its bun and shook it out. 'Oh don't worry, honey, I will. Come and help me so we can get out of here. You can stay at my place.'

'I'm fine—'

'I know I'm a bitch but I'm not going to send you home alone if you think some suit is following you.'

*

Marianne's apartment was an immaculate one-bedroom fortress overlooking St Kilda beach. I was probably the only person who didn't like the water view, but it was possible to forget about it once the black-out blinds were down. She'd moved in here while I'd been in Italy, eager to be on her own. She would never admit though that she lived beyond her means. Her apartment was in a complex with a rooftop gym and security gates, and not to mention the car loan she was paying off. She was determined though, to live the way she wanted. She was similar to me in that way – fighting the world for her independence. I liked to think I did so less violently than Marianne.

She showered while I raided her fridge. It was stocked with beer and wine and bottled water, but no food except for a mouldy cube of cheese on the top shelf. I took a bottle of water and sank into her plush sofa. The entire living area was white – the walls, the carpet, the furniture. Black and white framed photos on the walls, of her and her family mostly. A picture of me in the Alberto's kitchen, sitting on the bench with a shiny face and beer in hand.

Tucking up my legs, I leaned against the arm rest. The shower stopped in the bathroom and the door swung open. Marianne waltzed out, wrapped in a towel, her hair trailing wet over her shoulders. 'I thought you'd be asleep,' she said, and without waiting for an answer, slammed herself into her bedroom. I sipped from my water until she reappeared in her dressing gown and plopped down on the couch next to me. 'It's late,' she said, seizing my bottle and swigging from it. 'You want a shower or something?'

With a frown, I went back to the fridge and grabbed a second bottle of water. 'No, I'm okay.'

'You still think that guy was following you?'

Clenching my teeth, I joined her on the couch. 'Well, you certainly made me think twice about it.'

She narrowed her eyes. 'Don't be pissed.'

'Me? What's with *your* mood?'

She sighed. 'I don't like how you keep holding onto the shit that makes you unhappy.'

Here we go. 'What, like–'

'Like Marco,' she snapped, thumping the bottle on the coffee table.

I retaliated by slamming down my own unopened bottle. 'I haven't even mentioned him at all. I think you're the one that's hung up on him, since you're blaming him for every fucking little thing.'

'I'm the one with the mood?' she asked, with a small smile.

'Just say it. Say it.' I glared at her until her attempt at lightening the conversation melted away.

She wrapped her arms across her belly. 'Okay. I don't think there's a man following you. I think you're freaking out because you like Lucas and you're still not over Marco. You think every guy is going to fuck you up the way Marco did, so you shut out everyone else and think of any excuse you can not to get too close. And not just to men, but everyone, like, you won't even admit this to me.' She took a deep breath, puffing out her chest. 'I think you could be really happy if you let yourself relax. Lucas is a good guy and I keep trying to show you that not everyone is like Marco, and it's like banging my head against the wall.'

So there it was. Exactly what I'd assumed she was thinking, confirmed. 'Maybe you should stop trying then, and let me deal with things on my own. Did you think of that? Maybe you're more like my mother than you thought.' I waited for a flash of horror, or hurt, but she didn't react.

'Unlike your mother, I actually know who you are and

what you like. Tell me that Lucas isn't your type. Go.'

'I'm not going to argue with you. You *do* know me. But you push me so hard all the time. It's exhausting. My mother does that.'

She propped her feet on the coffee table, nudging her bottle aside with her toe. 'I guess she loves you too. In her own way.'

I let myself smile. 'So your pushiness comes from love?'

She smiled back. 'Of course. If I didn't love you, then I wouldn't give a fuck, would I?'

I sighed and leaned back against the couch.

Chapter 5

The next two days were uneventful, with no bearded man in sight, no drama. Marianne must have been right – it was another little freak-out of mine. Maybe I was nervous about getting closer to Lucas. I'd avoided Alberto's on purpose, not sure what the next step with Lucas would be, or should be.

The morning of my birthday, Marianne woke me early, hammering at the door.

'Breakfast,' she called. She'd brought coffee, pistachio biscotti, a bag of pears, and a bunch of pink lilies. 'Happy birthday, sugar.' She kissed my forehead and dragged a couple of chairs over to the bench.

'Thanks.' I grabbed a pear and sliced it on a saucer. 'I love these.' I sucked the juice from a sliver.

'I know.' She was filling a vase with water and arranging the flowers inside. 'So, how have you been? I haven't seen you for a couple of days.'

I took a sip of coffee. 'Yeah, I've been busy.'

She nodded, but her eyes were hard. She knew I'd been avoiding her. 'Everything okay? Haven't seen Mr Perfect around or ...'

'No,' I answered, taking another mouthful of coffee. 'Can we change the subject?'

She sat beside me, dusting yellow pollen from her hands. 'Okay.' She popped the lid off her coffee cup. 'Giovanni's made you a cake.'

'I had one the other day.'

'Yeah. He's in daddy mode though, let him go.' She took a bite of biscotti, crunching loudly. 'You know his rum cake. It's in the fridge already. He made it on Tuesday.'

'Oh God, okay. It's so good.'

'Hey, have you heard from Lucas lately?'

'Not since Monday. He said he'd see me tonight.'

'He was saying last night that Cam has four tickets for Sunday's game and thought we could go.'

'What game?'

'Football, honey.'

'Oh. Okay, yeah.'

She grinned. 'Can I give you a lift to work?'

I reached for another slice of pear. 'You better, being my birthday and all.'

*

No BMW, no bearded man in a coat holding out his phone. The narrow street was fairly quiet as I approached Alberto's. Parked cars. A distant murmur of a TV sitcom. Crisp, clear air I inhaled deep into my lungs.

Giovanni had closed the restaurant for my birthday. He let me in, dressed in his best suit and hair slicked back with his coconut cream. Behind him, the restaurant was lit with fairy lights. They'd been strung across the ceiling and above the bar. It looked straight out of a fairytale. I was glad I'd dressed up a bit, wearing my favourite black dress under Marianne's leather jacket. History had taught me Giovanni would make a fuss.

'You didn't have to close the restaurant tonight,' I said.

'I always do this for my family.'

My throat tightened a little. He clutched me against his tailored jacket and kissed my cheeks. Over his shoulder, I spotted Lucas sitting beside Cam and Marianne. He wore the usual white cotton shirt, but with jeans, his legs stretched out in front of him. One hand rested over his right knee, like it had been at the barbecue. *How often is he in pain with it?*

'*Carina,* how was your day? Did you have a cake already?'

'No,' I reassured Giovanni. I'd arrived at work that morning to find a second bunch of lilies on my desk, and a helium balloon tied to my chair. Karen had served me a cup of tea in my new mug – a present from her – which had my name painted in black over a large pink rose. It was kind of hideous, but still sweet, and she was proud to give me something I could leave on the desk.

'Good. I made the birthday cake.'

'I know, thank you.' I kissed his cheeks and he beamed. Tables had been dragged together, covered in a white cloth, red roses, and candles. The cake sat right in the centre, a huge white slab with a few candles scattered over the top, and Giovanni had even piped cream into roses around its edges. I'd seen him make this cake many times over the years for family members, and it was a ritual he took seriously. Marianne had joked in the past that he reserved the cream roses for his most cherished loved ones, and my cake had them.

I kissed him again. '*Sei un bell'uomo.*'

Giovanni and Luisa's family were crowded around the table. Little Oscar ran at me for a hug. I spotted Pete and his girlfriend, and Helena and Danni the waitresses. I embraced them all, got bombarded with kisses. Luisa passed me a flute of champagne, and when I turned, Lucas waited behind me. He hugged me, and as he pulled back, he said slowly, carefully, '*Buon compleanno.*'

'*Grazie,*' I answered, and we beamed at each other.

We ate Marianne's chicken, roasted vegetables and Luisa's Tuscan bread. I exchanged a few words with Lucas over the meal, but as soon as it was over, people wanted to talk to me and give me presents. I collected the gifts and hugs and kisses, and glasses of wine were passed constantly in my direction. So I stayed put, sipping from my glass, while everyone else changed seats and caught up with each other. Eventually, the cake was cut and I savoured the perfection of the corner piece – the creaminess and the booziness of it. Cam and I watched the kids dance between the tables, while Lucas made coffee with Luisa at the bar. I pointed out the kids to Cam, telling him their names and how they fit into the family. He seemed almost overwhelmed by it, shaking his head after meeting someone new. The sheer noise of Giovanni's family took time to get used to. In the early days, I used to go home with a headache.

Once I was drunk enough, I danced with the kids, standing them on chairs so we were the same height. They wrapped their little arms around me and chattered excitedly in my ear so I could hear them over the music. When the music changed into an unfamiliar, romantic slow song, I glanced over my shoulder and found Marianne nudging Lucas towards me. I clenched my teeth, realising everyone was in on it, clapping and cheering as Lucas walked over. I lowered Oscar from the chair and he skittered away, leaving Lucas and I alone on the makeshift dance floor.

'Not my idea,' Lucas said, and grimaced. He reached for my hand. I was drunk enough not to be embarrassed, but a flare of annoyance kept my jaw tight. I glared at Marianne, who had the decency to look guilty. 'I didn't argue though,' Lucas added, and I hid my smile, turning my face away from the audience.

We danced, moving slowly under the fairy lights. If it had been spontaneous, it would have been romantic, but instead, all the attention made it kind of crass.

'Feel like you're on display?' I asked him, not daring to gaze up into his face.

'Just a little bit,' he answered. 'I'd twirl you around or something, but I don't think my knee could handle it.'

The clapping continued, and as the song ended, I realised it wasn't only the Alberto's audience that had me feeling exposed. Lucas and I had been dancing right by the restaurant windows. I couldn't help but wonder who could be lurking outside in the dark, watching.

*

On Sunday, Marianne and I met Lucas and Cam at Flinders Street station. Cam waited proudly on the platform, his Blues jumper and scarf visible beneath his unzipped coat.

I pointed at his chest. 'Are you really wearing that?'

'You people,' he muttered. 'I don't understand people who

don't like footy.' He grabbed me around the shoulders and gave me a shake. 'You're an Aussie, come on!'

'No, it's just that I thought the Blues kind of sucked.'

Lucas burst out laughing. 'And we thought you didn't know anything about footy.'

I grinned up at him and my belly tightened a little; his nose was red with cold, his hands deep in his pockets. I hadn't seen him since our dance.

'You've got no choice, Amanda,' Cam said, walking me along the platform. 'If you're gonna barrack for the Tigers, you're not coming.'

'Give me a beer and I'll be fine,' I answered.

The train squealed to a stop. It was packed with supporters; clusters of navy blue and groups of yellow and black everywhere. We squeezed into the carriage, grabbing on to whatever we could. The train started up again, jerking back into action, nudging me back against Lucas. I stood very still, my shoulders against his chest, bracing my feet so I wouldn't slam back into him. A kid's backpack was jammed against my left leg, and a man that stunk of smoke too close in front, but it was Lucas who felt the closest. The train rocked our bodies closer together and by the time we reached Richmond station, I was crushed right up against him, holding my breath, feeling all his sharp angles and body heat. I couldn't even see Marianne and Cam until we spilled out onto the platform.

The MCG loomed huge and grey against the grey sky. I shivered in the chilly afternoon breeze. Cam and Marianne caught up to us, Marianne now wearing Cam's scarf. I raised my eyebrows at her.

'You right, mate?' Cam eyed Lucas, who shook his head

dismissively.

'Is your knee hurting?' Marianne asked. I hadn't mentioned anything to Marianne, but wasn't surprised that she knew already. She always managed to find out whatever she needed to know about anyone.

'I'll be right once I sit down. Just standing on the train–'

'That's probably my fault. I kept bumping up against you.' I gave his hand a squeeze.

'Nah, I didn't mind that.'

Marianne shrieked with laughter, throwing her arm around me. I tried not to react as we queued up at the gates.

*

The Blues won. I was cold and stiff from sitting on the plastic seat for so long, but the beer helped to take the edge off. I went walking with Lucas a few times, so he could stretch out his leg. He told me he had trouble sitting in the same position, but from half time onwards he seemed okay – I guess the beer helped to ease his discomfort.

Cam's devotion to the Blues was contagious. I'd never been interested in football before, and had only been to a game once, but found myself caught up in the excitement whenever Carlton scored a goal. At one stage, half-pissed, I'd asked Lucas, shouting over the noise, 'So, a goal is six points, right?' resulting in everyone laughing uproariously. I paid close attention until the next goal then studied the scoreboard until I got my answer.

After the game, we went back to my place with the plan to order pizza. Aware that Lucas, or Cam for that matter, had never been there, I tried to remember if I'd cleaned up before leaving for the footy. It wouldn't have mattered so much except that my tiny studio apartment was so small, anyone standing at the door could see the whole damn place, and with nothing but a curtain dividing the bedroom from the lounge area, I had nowhere to hide my crap, unless I shoved it in the linen cupboard outside the bathroom.

I unlocked the door and let everyone inside. I had made the bed and tidied the lounge room. And thank God, clothes weren't strewn around everywhere as if I was in high school and had been trying on every possible outfit before a date. The kitchen was a bit of a mess, the dishes weren't done, but there were never many – I rarely cooked for myself.

Cam went straight to the couch, bombing down into it. Marianne fetched a couple of beers from my fridge and joined him. Lucas, though, stood on the spot and gazed around.

Cam was raving about some football player who'd kicked lots of goals, his commentary punctuated by the sound of his beer opening. *Pssst.* Then Marianne's. *Pssst.*

'I like your place,' Lucas said. His eyes settled on my coffee machine. He headed to it, running a hand along its chrome surface. He restacked the espresso cups I'd tossed on top of it and turned with a grin. 'This is magnificent.'

'I believe you.' I leaned against the bench beside him.

'May I?' His fingers twitched at the switches. 'I'll be gentle.'

'Yes.' I passed him the bag of beans from the cupboard above and he took a whiff. Nodded.

He adjusted to the new machine like a true expert, grinding the beans while the machine heated, running the water through and tamping the coffee. His hands were perfect, I noticed. Smooth and tanned, long fingers with short, rounded nails. As I watched him use my machine, it was becoming more and more difficult not to like him. I hadn't been in this situation for over two years, and it was awkward and uncomfortable. Last time hadn't exactly been a successful love story.

Marianne and Cam had fallen silent. Their commentary of the game had stopped and they were watching us, standing side by side at my kitchen bench. They both paid close attention, their faces alight. Marianne met my eyes and everything I'd been thinking became available to her as though I'd been typing a transcript. She didn't grin, or make a face, but her expression softened. She was turning to mush in a relieved, motherly, proud kind of way, and it made me more nervous.

Lucas held out his hand, a short black cradled in his palm. I took it and sipped slowly. He sipped his too and we stood there in silence, the awkwardness heavy in the room. I shot a look at Marianne, who opened her mouth and resumed effortless conversation with Cam. I wished I could do the same with Lucas – open my mouth and spill words, but my head was filled with doubt. Lucas, in general, seemed a much more relaxed person than me, but even he focused intently on his cup.

'Do you use this every day?' he finally asked.

'The machine? Yeah.' *This is agony.*

'I'm still shopping for one. But this might have me convinced though.'

'What do you use at home now?'

He bit his lip then muttered, 'Instant. I make instant.'

'Are you kidding me?' I cried. 'You're a barista. Shame on

you.'

'Yeah, I know, it's sad.' He smiled and drained his cup. 'But I don't usually drink coffee at home. That's my excuse, anyway.' He took my empty cup and went to the sink, where he ran the tap, and holding both cups in the stream of water, washed them clean using his fingers. 'What are you doing tomorrow?' he asked, with his back to me.

'Working,' I answered. My body buzzed. Maybe just the caffeine, but I steadied myself anyway, leaning back against the bench.

'I have the day off if you want to catch up after.' He turned over the wet cups to drain on the sink. 'I can meet you somewhere if you want.' He crossed his arms and faced me. There was a challenge in the gesture, and I swallowed. He was saying it again – *if you want* – leaving it up to me.

'Okay.'

He came closer, hesitating only inches away. His gaze was intense and I tried not to flinch.

'Listen,' I said, keeping my voice low. 'There's one thing you need to know about me. Maybe my spokesperson Marianne has shared this with you already, but ... I freak out really easily. Just so you know.'

He cocked his head to the side, studying me. He was silent a moment. 'I'll do my best not to freak you out.'

I nodded. 'Thanks. We don't really know each other, that's all.' I made myself smile, but the realisation churned my stomach. I shouldn't be so drawn to someone I'd just met, someone I barely knew.

He smiled back. 'Well, sometimes things happen like this, I guess.'

True. It had happened to me before.

He took a step closer, but hesitated again. I took the opportunity to free myself from the moment, and reached for my mobile to call for pizza.

*

'You know, Amanda does have her patriotic moments,' Marianne said. She peeled a slice of salami off her pizza and popped it in her mouth.

'Just not with footy,' Cam interrupted.

'No, no, she doesn't follow the AFL. But recently,' she grinned, glancing at me, 'at a karaoke bar–'

'No,' I cried, throwing a cushion at her. 'Don't you dare tell that story!'

'Which story?' she mocked. 'You mean the story of you slamming tequila shots and then singing *Khe Sanh?*

Cam roared with laughter. 'So, you don't know your Aussie Rules, but you know your Cold Chisel.'

'Everyone knows Cold Chisel,' I answered. 'It's in-born.'

'It actually was a beautiful moment. She can really sing when she's pissed. She had everyone singing along.'

'Tequila,' I said, shaking my head. 'Does it every time.'

'Do you have any here?' Lucas asked. 'I'd like to see that.'

Through the laughter, I settled back on the couch and took a mouthful of pizza. 'Never again. It made me so sick that night.'

'Oh, that's right.' Marianne grimaced. 'Worth it for the memory though. I wish I'd filmed it.'

*

It was getting late when everyone left. Marianne and Cam were drunk, clomping down the stairs ahead of Lucas and me. The taxi waited at the kerb, headlights blurring the fog, radio humming news through the window.

'You call me or I'll call you?' Lucas asked, as we followed Marianne and Cam down the stairs. Marianne was shrieking and giggling at something Cam was saying.

'I don't know. I'll call you after work.'

'Okay.'

We were both tipsy, and in my case the beer had helped dispel some of my nervousness. At the bottom of the stairs, as I reached to drag the door open, Lucas grabbed for my hand. I let him pull me back, framing me in the frozen rectangle of the doorway. He pulled me against him and kissed me. His lips were warm and soft, and when his tongue found mine, I sank into him, sliding my arms around his hips.

From the taxi, I could hear Marianne squealing and Cam hollering. Lucas turned his back to them, using his body to shield me from the road and their view. That gesture alone pushed Marco a little further into the background. I slipped a hand underneath his jacket, his shirt, until my fingers grazed his skin. He held me tighter. The cool air was tinged with the smell of exhaust, but the smell of Lucas was stronger. Coffee. The beans from the restaurant, the beans from my cupboard upstairs.

'You smell like coffee,' I murmured.

'Hmmm?'

'You smell good.'

A tiny moan buzzed in his throat. 'Do you want me to stay?'

'I want you to ...' I whispered.

His face was expectant. 'But not tonight?'

I shook my head.

His gaze softened. 'Okay.' He brushed his lips across my cheek. 'I'll see you tomorrow.'

As he walked to the car, I stood and watched, leaning back against the door to keep it open. Marianne and Cam jostled him in the back of the taxi like excited teenagers, and amongst the chaos, he raised his hand in a goodbye. I waved back, and as the car disappeared up the street, I allowed myself to really smile.

*

Back in my apartment, I stripped off as I walked to the bedroom, peeling off my jeans and throwing them as I went. I pulled on an extra-large jumper and tied up my hair. Crawling onto the bed, I wished Lucas was here with me. But I couldn't do it. Not yet. Marco still lurked in my unconscious somewhere, still reared his head while I slept. I didn't know how to get rid of him, but tonight, I didn't much care. Something had shifted. I wasn't scared of Lucas; he was different. I liked him, I couldn't deny it. And I wasn't going to pretend that I didn't anymore.

I lifted the corner of the window blind and peered down into the street. The place where Lucas and I had stood only minutes earlier was empty now, with nothing but a sickly orange glow from the streetlight left behind. My breath fogged the window pane; I wiped it away. Something seemed ... off, and it took me a minute to realise what it was.

Across the street, a man in a long coat stood alone in the dark, beside the house directly opposite my window. Fog hung in the air, shielding him, wrapping around him so I couldn't see him clearly. But the white blur of his face was pointed in my direction, partly covered with a dark shadow of beard.

An icy chill crept up my spine, replacing the memory of Lucas and his warm hands, his hot breath. It looked like the same man from the restaurant; the man who had taken a picture of me.

Oh my God ...

Dropping the blind, I lowered myself out of sight. With my belly flat to the mattress, I covered my face with my hands and squeezed. I dug my fingers into the skin until I could feel the imprint of my nails.

Why?

I wasn't insane. I wasn't losing it. There really was a man out there on the street ... but was it the same man? It couldn't be. A lot of men wore coats. A lot of men had beards.

I slithered back into my jeans and grabbed my keys. I had to find out. I had to go down to the street and see. But at the door, I stopped. What if it was him? If it really was, then that meant he'd followed me home.

With a groan, I dropped my keys on the kitchen bench. Fastening the chain on the door, I pressed my ear against it for a moment. I couldn't hear anyone creeping about out there.

My phone beeped and I went to it. A text message there from Marianne. *So exciting! Speak to u in morn xx*

I knew I couldn't call her, couldn't tell her I was afraid. After the way she'd acted at Alberto's, she'd probably laugh. Or worse, blame my insecurity over Lucas.

My breath rasped loudly in the quiet room. I surveyed

my surroundings. Everything was in place.

The pizza boxes stacked on the kitchen bench, empty bottles clustered beside them.

A vase held my birthday lilies, now starting to wilt.

The espresso cups upturned on the sink.

The coffee machine sat quietly now, gleaming silver under the kitchen light.

Squeezing the phone in my fist, I tiptoed over to the bed. The blind was down but I ached to lift it back up and check if he was still down there. Instead, I perched on the edge of the mattress, rubbing my wet palms against my jeans.

This was not some psychological coping mechanism because I felt nervous about getting involved with someone. No. This was something else. There was a shaky feeling in my chest that something wasn't right, a primitive sense of doom.

My mother's voice taunted: *You're in a building with no security. What if someone breaks in? A rapist could walk right up to your door.*

I shook my head. From where the bed was positioned against the wall, I could see the whole apartment. It was directly opposite the door. I stared hard at it.

The knob was still.

The chain was fastened.

I was being stupid.

Chapter 6

Lucas stands on the balcony, his hair catching the salty breeze. He's looking out to sea, his white work sleeves rolled up to the elbows. The water is calm as he waits for me. Walking along the road towards him, I'm not afraid. The sun is hot. It soaks into my bones and makes me feel more alive than I've felt for years. It's time. He's the one. I absolutely know it. The knowledge is a bubble that drifts along in front of me, leading me to him. I'm not afraid. I call his name.

Lucas turns. It's not him at all, but Marco. Wearing a coat. His face pale. No, it's not Marco. It's the man with the beard, and he's smiling at me. He beckons me closer, come to me, come to me ... he has something to tell me. I try to escape, but the ground is shaking. The road pulls away from the side of the cliff, splitting, crumbling.

As I fall, he stands on the balcony and waves.

*

I left for work at dawn.

First light soothed me, when the streets were quiet. The air was brisk and seemed cleaner, cooling my lungs when I sucked it in. I didn't even want to think about waiting for a tram. Work was close enough that I could walk the whole way, even if it took me a while. It didn't matter. I didn't want to wait. I didn't want to stop and stand still. The thought of it made my heart thump, as if I'd be stolen away by giant hands.

So I walked, feeling an inexplicable sense of guilt and anger. My mother hated where I lived, and had killed the excitement of having my own place at last. My little rented apartment wasn't much, but it was independence and freedom after the rough landing I'd had from Italy. Marco had left open wounds and I'd patched them up by finding my own little nest.

Last night was the first time I'd ever felt unsafe in my apartment.

I swore as I walked, so angry with myself. The freezing morning wasn't doing what it should; I couldn't clear my head. My boots thumped against the footpath, each step jolting, my bag bouncing. Marianne's text remained unanswered because I couldn't figure out what to say. I was supposed to see Lucas today, but I didn't know what to do about that either. I'd have to call him later, if he didn't call me first. After a night of messy sleep tangled by ugly dreams, everything seemed too complicated. My head was too full.

But the thought that dominated all the others was that of the bearded man. Mr Perfect. If indeed that had been him outside my building last night, what the hell did he want with me?

*

I made it through the morning, sleepwalking my way through the hours, and somehow managing to do it with a smile for the patients. Karen kept her distance, not asking me any questions. Maybe she sensed the bad mood simmering below my practiced customer-service bullshit persona.

At lunch, I sat alone in the kitchen. It was rare; usually a doctor or nurse or student shared the table. I felt blessed. I peeled a banana and chewed it, my eyes closed and my head down.

'Hi Amanda.'

Shit.

'Hi, Dr Kim.'

'Isn't it quiet? Glorious.'

I nodded, flicking my banana peel into the bin. Dr Kim sat opposite, sipping from his favourite mug.

'You seem under the weather today.'

'I haven't been sleeping very well, that's all.' I took a sip of coffee. Cold and bitter.

'It is flu season–'

'I'm not sick.' I smiled at him. 'Just tired.'

'Something troubling you? I'm a good listener.'

I nudged my cup away. 'I don't know.' I sighed, too exhausted to think up a lie. 'I have bad dreams.'

'Oh?'

'Yeah, stupid dreams. Not all the time, but last night was one of those nights.'

'Have you considered counselling? There might be a reason. Is it the same dream?'

'Sort of.' I tried to smile at him, but his face was so concerned I had to look away. 'I'm okay though, really.'

'I could give you something to help you sleep, but that

doesn't exactly fix the problem.'

'No thanks,' I sighed again. 'I don't want to take anything.' Pushing my chair back, I stood.

'Well, you know where to find me if you want to talk.' His thin fingers toyed with his mug, his small frame barely filling the chair.

'Thanks, Dr Kim.'

*

Only a handful of patients sat in the waiting room, and phone calls were few and far between. I took the opportunity to get away from the desk, retreating to the file room where patient records had been dumped in a tray to be re-filed. The room wasn't really a room, but an area partitioned off from the foyer, so patients couldn't see the filing cabinets. Not the most secure set-up, but for a small clinic there weren't many options.

It didn't take long to clear the tray of the morning's records. I decided to clean the cabinets, finally wipe off those old marker stains, and maybe even dust the shelves above while I was at it. I'd only gotten through one when the phones started ringing. The afternoon rush we called it; where people tried to get appointments for the following day. Karen had the receiver under her chin and was waving at me with her free hand. I went to relieve her, slipping back into my seat and reaching for my own phone. The sliding doors by the desk parted, and I glanced up. A mother and young daughter walked in holding hands, but it wasn't them that caught my attention. Behind them, outside the clinic, a man leant against the fence.

It was him.

Slick dark hair, dark beard, eyes like blackened marbles pointed right at me.

No doubt this time.

As the doors slid closed, I continued to stare through the glass. He really was looking at me. He wasn't looking away. He wasn't moving.

My hand hovered above the bleating telephone. To my left, I heard Karen whisper my name.

I'd been right. He *had* been following me. The bastard *had* been at my place last night. I jumped out of my chair, sending it shooting back into the partition. My heart thumping, I stalked outside, where he stood alone. His foot was braced against the fence, his arms crossed. He wasn't much taller than me, but his eyes were cold. Pure hate shone from them.

God, what am I doing?

'Who are you?' My voice was steady and I lifted my chin, trying to appear defiant, even though my chest felt constricted, my breath coming short and fast. But I'd had enough. I had to know, if only to show Marianne I wasn't losing it.

'My name is Graham Coates.' His voice was flat and he spoke slowly, carefully, as though speaking to a child.

'Why are you following me?'

'That's a good question, Amanda. But I think you should ask your *boyfriend* to answer that one.' The shadow of a sneer passed over his face.

'What?'

'Lucas Williams. Ask Lucas who I am.' He turned and walked slowly down the driveway towards the car park at the rear of the clinic.

'Hey,' I called after him. 'How do you know who I am?'

He didn't respond. I waited until he'd disappeared around the corner then ran inside. I fumbled for my bag under the desk. The fury rose like lava inside me.

'Amanda, what are you doing?' Karen snapped over the shriek of the telephone. Ignoring her, I ran into the kitchen. Warm with the remnants of lunch; the smell of instant noodles and stale coffee hung in the air. Stripes of afternoon sun cut through the venetian blinds, slashing yellow across the floor. I went to the window. The car park was mostly empty. I couldn't see his car. I dialled Lucas's number, slapping my shaking hand hard against my thigh as it rang.

'Hey, how's it going?'

'Where are you?' I demanded. 'Are you at work?'

A pause. 'Uh, no I have the day off, remember?'

'Where are you?' I asked again, my voice quivering. Just when I was starting to relax and believe that things could work with Lucas. Just when I thought things could be different. Different to Marco. Just when I thought there might actually be a chance of an easy, no bullshit–

'I'm at home. What's wrong?'

'I need to talk to you. No, I need to see you now.'

'I can meet you. Or you can come here if you want. You have my address.'

'No, I don't.'

'Marianne put it in your phone yesterday, remember? What's wrong?' he repeated.

What's wrong? What's wrong? You've got some guy stalking me, that's what's wrong. I wanted to scream: *Who the fuck are you?*

'I'm coming over,' I said into the phone.

I collided with Dr Kim in the hallway. 'Amanda, slow down.'

'I'm sorry, Dr Kim, but I have to go.'

'What's wrong?' He must have seen my panic. 'Can I drive you somewhere?'

'No, I have to go. I'll talk to you later. I'm so sorry.'

*

The taxi pulled up outside a white weatherboard house – plain and ugly and bordered with low, bare shrubs. I paid the driver, asking him to wait. I sucked in my breath sharp and hard. No cars were parked in the driveway or out the front, but somehow I'd half-expected to see a black BMW parked there. I walked towards the front porch, stepping over cracks with weeds snaking through.

Lucas met me at the door. His hair was out, long and stringy to his shoulders. His jeans were faded and ripped. For the first time, I didn't like him. I didn't trust the concern on his face or his hand guiding me by the shoulder into his lounge room. The room was old and breathlessly warm. Two sagging couches faced a dark television. I dropped my bag on one. A guitar leant against the wall, and an archway led into a kitchen dominated by a wooden table and vinyl-covered chairs.

'What's happening?'

I spotted his phone on the coffee table, resting on top of a pile of folded newspapers.

'Graham Coates came to my work today.'

The colour drained from his face. His lips parted, but he

didn't say anything.

'Who is he?' I asked. I found myself adopting Graham Coates's slow, careful tone.

'He's the man who hit me in my car six months ago,' he said, his voice hushed.

That threw me. I stared up at him, shaking my head. I wanted to touch him, but my brain screamed, keeping me a few paces away. I didn't understand, and I needed to. 'What happened in that accident?'

Lucas met my eyes with that same dark expression I'd seen at the barbecue, the one I hadn't been able to read. 'His wife was killed.'

My knees buckled and I dropped onto the nearest couch. There really was no air in this room. 'Oh my God,' I gasped.

His expression was pleading. 'He blamed me. He said it was my fault, but it wasn't. It wasn't my fault.'

'He's been following me!'

'What?' Lucas sat beside me, gripping my arm. 'What do you mean?'

'He's been following me,' I repeated, my voice a little louder, a little higher. 'He knows my name. He knows where I work.' I exhaled. 'He knows where I live.' I pulled away from his grip and stood.

'He knows where ...?'

'He was there last night. After you left, I saw him from my window.'

Lucas stood too, swiping a hand across his face. 'We should call the police or something.'

'Oh, this is just great.'

'He threatened me in the hospital.'

'What?'

'After the accident. He came into my room and was screaming about how it was my fault. I'd just had surgery and I couldn't even move, and he ...' Lucas braced his hands on his head, closing his eyes. His face was so pale. 'I said sorry, because he was so upset, and so angry, and of course I was upset too. I mean, she died, so I said sorry, even though the accident wasn't my fault. I was driving, and his car crossed into my lane. I couldn't stop it. She was thrown from the car.'

I paced the length of the lounge room on trembling legs. The images flickered in my head: two cars colliding, a woman crashing through the windscreen, Lucas hurt and bleeding. I stood in the archway to the kitchen, where clean dishes were laid out over checked tea towels. A bowl of overripe bananas sat on top of the old Kelvinator fridge.

'He's been following you too?' I finally asked.

He shook his head. 'I don't think so. I don't know.'

I rubbed at my eyes. A headache bloomed there, spreading across into my temples. Where could I go? If he knew where I lived, where I worked, about Alberto's ...

'Well, he must be following you.' I spun to him. 'I've seen him at the restaurant three times. That's where I first saw him. It was only after that, after the football last night when we kissed at my place ...' *Lucas* led him to me. It had nothing to do with my mother at all. I wanted to scream. 'I have to go. My taxi's waiting.' I strode towards the door, scooping my bag from the couch.

'Amanda, don't. Stay here and we'll work out what to do.'

'You know what? You work it out. This is your mess. You can take care of it.'

He blocked the doorway. 'I can't take care of it without you. You have to tell the cops what he said to you, what he—'

'I can't deal with this shit!'

'Trust me, if we call the police now–'

'Trust you?' I snapped, hating my voice. Hating myself, but unable to control my simmering anger. 'I've known you for a week and now I have a psycho following me!'

'You can trust me. You can.' His eyes were wide, desperate. 'I know all of this is because of me, and I'm sorry, but we have to go to the police together. Come on,' he reached out for me, but I pulled away.

'I have to go. My taxi's waiting,' I repeated.

He clenched his jaw, and when he spoke next it was through gritted teeth. 'What did Marco do to you that was so fucking bad?'

The words were like a kick to the stomach. 'Fuck you. This has nothing to do with him.'

'Yes, it does! You don't trust me, and you're flinching away from me all the time. It's like I can't even talk to you unless I get a written invitation first.'

I pushed him, hard. He stumbled back against the door. 'Get out of the way,' I shouted. Without another word, he stepped aside and I wrenched the door open. I ran out to the taxi, not looking back.

Chapter 7

My mind raced as the taxi driver headed back towards the clinic. It wasn't even 3pm but I didn't want Graham Coates to be there when I returned. I didn't want to go home either. What if he was waiting for me there? As the taxi crept closer to work, I broke into a sweat. I told the driver to stop, and ran to the next tram I could see. Without bothering to check where it headed, I jumped on and buried myself in the closest empty seat.

I stepped off at Bourke Street, into crowds and noise. Surrounding myself with strangers, I relaxed. My muscles loosened, my heart rate slowed. The crush of pedestrians moved at a snail's pace, but I didn't care. Finally I was shielded, protected. I breathed them in – cigarette smoke and different fabrics and flowing hair and bags swinging against hips. This tapestry of little lives was my armour.

Without a plan, I shuffled blindly along the pavement. A group had gathered around a busker playing "Sweet Thing" and I stood with them. A gravelly voice and eyes closed, he seemed oblivious to those who watched. His version was so close to the real thing that I could have cried, but instead, I backed away, heading through the doors of the Myer building.

Around me, well-dressed people were escaping the chilly afternoon. The swish of a trench coat caught my eye and I flinched. Nowhere was safe. I had nowhere to hide. Not really. Not anymore. But with people around me, I wasn't alone.

I rode the escalator up towards the huge domed ceiling, glittering glass like icicles above my head. I didn't know where I was going but moved faster now, climbing the steps as they scrolled higher.

At Brunetti's, I ordered a latte and cannoli. I found a table right in the entrance, where I could sit with my back to one of the cake fridges. I scanned the cafe as I sipped my coffee. Why had Lucas said that about Marco? Didn't we have more important things to worry about? Like the man who was following me. *We* ... Well, I guess I *was* attached to Lucas now, whether I wanted to be or not. A psycho was following me, closing in, narrowing my avenues of escape. Safety could only be found in a place like this – public, busy, and loud.

Tapping my foot, I surveyed my surroundings. I had the right to feel safe and comfortable in the places I loved, like my home, and my work, and Alberto's – my second home. After two years licking the wounds Marco had left behind, I'd finally allowed myself to consider another relationship, only to find that Lucas was carrying his own giant bag of drama. I was too, but I was healing, ready to start over. Wasn't I? I'd thought Lucas safe, reliable, easy. But it was happening all over again.

Wasn't there such a thing as an easy relationship? Giovanni and Luisa were like two halves of one person, just like the old cliché. Even my parents were effortless together. Dad wasn't fazed by my mother's annoying personality traits, because he clearly loved her enough. I guess it was a sign things weren't going to work out with Lucas, just as they hadn't with Marco. But already Lucas was a part of the Alberto's family, and I wasn't sure how I could possibly cut him out of my life now without leaving scars.

I swallowed back tears.

Damn him. Damn it all.

*

I rounded the corner into my street.

'Did you talk to him?'

My head snapped up. Graham Coates was leaning casually against the wall of my building, partially lit by the streetlight.

Anger surged through my body, making me shake. I'd been out for hours, and it still wasn't safe for me to come home. I'd waited for darkness to fall, but that hadn't made any difference. How long had he been here? I was tired, my feet sore, and I wanted to go upstairs to bed. And I had a *right* to do so. Fury bubbled like acid up my throat.

'Is this your job now, is it? Following me around, waiting for me?' I snapped.

He straightened, surprised. 'You're part of the plan, Amanda.'

'Yeah, what's that? To get back at someone you think killed your wife?' I dropped my gaze to his left hand. Sure enough, a ring glinted under the streetlight.

'*He* caused the accident. Not me. *It wasn't me.*' His deliberate tone was gone. So was the coldness in his voice. He could have been any man tortured by grief. I almost started to relax, when I remembered what Lucas said about him coming to the hospital.

'I'm sorry about what happened to your wife. But it doesn't have anything to do with me.'

I waited for him to reply.

'I hardly know Lucas,' I urged. 'I don't want to get involved in this.'

He stared. Slowly, he smiled.

My heart hammered against my ribcage.

My eyes flicked to the right. The BMW was there, waiting.

He dove forward, snatching me by the wrists.

'No!' I tried to yank my arms free.

He pushed me against the wall, and cracked my head backwards against the bricks. Pain exploded. *Fireworks.* I fell forward into his chest, unable to do anything but gasp for air. My handbag lay discarded near my feet. I couldn't reach it. I opened my mouth to scream, but my voice wasn't there. He wrapped his arms around my waist and carried me toward his car.

The click of the door handle.

The flash of the interior light.

No! No! No!

On instinct, I kicked up my feet, twisting my body until I was able to brace them against the side of his car. Pain tore up my back. I pushed down as hard as I could with my feet, straightening my legs, until I heard him grunt.

'Get in the fucking car,' he growled.

I pushed again.

His beard scratched my neck.

He smelled of sweat.

'Get in, you little bitch!'

I thrashed again, until I was dumped in the gutter beside the car. He squatted in front of me, backlit by the orange streetlight.

'We are going to get in the car,' he panted, anger clipping his words. 'And we are going to pick up your boy, so when I cut your throat he can watch you die.'

His fist slammed into my face. Clanging filled my ears. My vision swam. His fingers dug into my arms and he shook me like a rag doll. Shoved me deeper into the gutter. Filthy water soaked through my pants, into my hair. Pain screamed through my body. I fought to stay awake, but darkness was closing in.

I'm going to die.

*

I sat on the couch with a blanket around my shoulders. My clothes were dirty and wet. I should have been cold, but I wasn't. Everything hurt, yet I felt numb. *How is that possible?* A female paramedic knelt before me, tending to my injuries and asking questions I immediately forgot.

In the kitchen, two police officers chatted to my neighbour. He lived across the street, and I'd seen him walking his dog occasionally, but I'd never spoken to him before. I didn't know his name. But tonight he'd saved my life, chasing away Graham Coates and carrying me upstairs.

Although I'd babbled words of gratitude, how could I thank someone properly for saving my life?

Marianne sat beside me, prompting me to speak when I fell silent. A light shone into my eyes, its beam flashing from side to side. Clipboards. Uniforms. Phones. Everyone talking, their faces contorted with shock and anger. My apartment full of people. Noise. So much noise.

My mother was right about one thing: my apartment was small. Swollen with voices, faces. Bursting at the seams.

Lucas and Cam arrived, and while Cam stopped to speak to the cops, Lucas came to me, pale and wide-eyed. I didn't even want to know what I looked like.

'I'm *so* sorry,' he said. His voice was a gentle rumble that remained distinct from all the others. I released one stiff hand from the blanket and held it out. He took it, reached for the other one. 'My God, look at you,' he murmured, and his lower lip trembled.

'I don't want to know,' I whispered. 'Lucas, he wants to kill me. He wants you to see me die.'

His expression told me he already knew that. Someone had told him exactly what had happened. 'That's *not* going to happen.'

'I tried to fight. He tried to get me in the car.'

'I know.'

'It would have worked too. If my neighbour hadn't come ...'

'I know.' He exhaled a shaky breath. 'I'm sorry about earlier. I shouldn't have said that.'

'I shouldn't have left.'

The paramedic touched my knee. 'I think you should go to the hospital to get your head checked out.'

I blinked at her. 'Why, what's wrong with me?'

She seemed younger than me, possibly inexperienced. But she was calm, businesslike. 'With a head injury, it's a good idea to be monitored for a while to make sure everything's okay.'

Marianne leaned over me. 'How much does it hurt?'

The pain slammed against the sides of my skull when I moved. Like blades, nicking the back of my eyes. Like lightning, shooting jagged through the sky. Nausea swirled in my gut, and the thought of emptying my stomach felt like it would be the only thing that would make me feel better.

Concern was etched into Marianne, Lucas and the paramedic's faces as they waited for me to reply. 'It's like a bad headache, I guess.'

'Do you want to go to the hospital?' Marianne pressed.

I tried to shake my head, but gasped. 'I want to ... go to sleep. I want to ...'

'Is it safe for her to sleep?' Lucas asked the paramedic, who nodded.

'Amanda needs to be monitored for the next twelve hours or so. This is best done at hospital.'

The male policeman came over and squatted beside the paramedic, his eyes latching onto mine. 'We'll be patrolling the neighbourhood tonight, Amanda. If you want to stay home, we won't be far away.'

The paramedic glared at him. 'Look, I'm just trying to do my job here–'

'I want to stay home,' I interrupted. 'I just want to go to sleep. Is that okay?'

The paramedic pursed her lips. 'You need to have someone

staying with you.'

'I'll be here,' Marianne said.

The paramedic began to pack up her things.

'I can clean her up now, right?' Marianne asked. She took my hand and helped me stand, then leading me slowly towards the bathroom, she closed the door behind us. 'Okay, listen,' she said gently. Her voice was so quiet she didn't even sound like herself. Instantly, I was on guard. 'You're going to get a shock when you see your face, but it's not as bad as it looks.'

'What do you mean?'

'You've got blood on your face–'

'What?'

'It's just from your nose, honey.' She put her hands on my shoulders. 'You're okay. The paramedic said you'll be fine, but you've got a bump on your head and you will bruise here.' With the tip of a finger she touched my cheekbone. Hot pain bloomed under my eye and I flinched. When she moved aside, I looked into the mirror.

Blood had collected on my top lip, over my chin and on the collar of my shirt.

'Oh, fuck him,' I whispered.

'That's my girl.' Marianne had wet a washcloth and leaned against the sink. She wiped my face gently, stopping every few seconds to rinse it out. When she'd finished, my face was damp and clean. My nose and cheek were swollen and red, and a slash of blue had already begun to sprout beneath my eye.

'Let's get these wet things off.' Marianne removed my blazer, slinging it over the shower rail. Apart from the droplets decorating my collar like rosebuds, my shirt was almost dry underneath. She crouched and helped me out of my boots, then peeled off my sodden socks.

When we emerged, the paramedic was gone. Cam was shouting at the male policeman, while the other cop tried to calm him down.

'What the fuck are you doing? You know who he is, go get him!'

The cop saw me, and ignoring Cam, pointed to my notepad on the kitchen bench. 'We'll be back in the morning,' he said to me. 'We'll need to ask you some more questions once you've had some rest. But please call overnight if you need.'

'So, will you let us know if you find Coates or what?' Cam asked, his voice rough and angry.

'Yes, of course,' the female officer said. 'We have all the details we need. And we'll be patrolling the neighbourhood tonight, but if anything else happens, call right away.'

'Do they think we're fucking stupid?' Cam snapped, once the door had closed behind them.

'You should get some sleep,' Lucas said, from where I'd left him on the couch. His face still had that pasty look, like he was on the verge of passing out.

I fingered the piece of paper on the bench. *Constable Jason Richards.* As much as I craved sleep, I wasn't sure I'd be able to. I tried to shake my head. Throbbing pain rocketed through my skull.

'I still think it would've been a good idea to take her to hospital,' said Cam. He paced like a caged lion.

'A hospital hasn't stopped him before.' Lucas leaned forward, holding his own head in his hands.

'She'll be fine here,' said Marianne, blocking Cam's path.

'I'm staying. You'll stay too, right, Lucas?'

'Yeah.'

'What if she has a concussion?' Cam argued.

'She's okay; no sign of that. We just have to keep an eye on her.' Marianne held Cam's arms, physically halting his relentless pacing.

'I'm right here, you know. Don't talk about me like ...' I supported my head with a hand on each side, willing the pain to stop.

Marianne moved to the kitchen sink and filled a glass with water. She popped two small white tablets into my palm. 'The paramedic left these. Swallow. And you should take a shower now, before they kick in.'

I didn't argue, walking back into the bathroom and peeling off the rest of my clothes. Standing under the hot water, I tried not to cower from the needle-like spray.

My head was so tender that it hurt to even touch my scalp, but I desperately wanted to wash my hair. I settled for shampooing the ends, and leaned against the tiles, knowing that for a couple of minutes at least, I was concealed behind my mildewed shower curtain. Over the sound of the shower, I couldn't hear the others, but I knew they were out there. I knew that for now, I was safe.

Finally I felt warm and clean. But when I stepped out onto the bath mat, the snap of cold brought me back. I shivered. My legs started to shake. Marianne brought me pyjama pants, an extra-large "I LOVE ROMA" T-shirt that I wore to bed. She collected the pile of wet clothes from the floor and led me out, where Cam waited on the other side of the door. He hugged me, gentler than I thought him capable.

'I'll see you tomorrow.'

'Okay,' I whispered, wobbling on my feet. The drugs were kicking in.

'Lucas said I can go with Cam and he'll stay with you,' Marianne said, passing Cam my wet clothes.

I blinked through the drug haze. 'What?'

Marianne held my shoulders. 'They're strong painkillers. By the time you wake up it'll be morning, and then the police will be back to take care of this.' There was that soft voice again. Beneath the blur of the painkillers, the rattly feeling was back in my chest.

'I think you should stay,' I whispered to her, unable to process how close Lucas was and whether he could hear me or not.

'Okay,' she nodded. I was starting to float, and her face didn't look quite right. 'You don't have to worry about anything. Get some rest.' She moved me past Lucas, where he was arranging a blanket and pillow on the couch, and led me to my bed. I crawled underneath the covers. The clock on the bedside table glowed 8:22. It took me a few seconds to realise that only a couple of hours had passed since I'd arrived home and found Graham Coates waiting.

'Get some sleep,' Marianne whispered, kissing my forehead.

I closed my eyes.

Chapter 8

I woke on my back, the apartment dark and quiet. A dreamless sleep. I moved my head gingerly. The pain had eased. *Drugs.* The drugs were good.

Marianne was beside me, her head back and mouth open wide, snoring – a soft, gasping sound I'd heard many times over the years.

I rolled onto my side carefully, blinking to clear my vision. Lucas was stretched out on my couch, his hair trailing over the arm rest. The only light in the apartment was the glow of the television where a muted episode of *Frasier* beamed in. I glanced at the clock: 3:41. I'd had a full night's sleep already, yet it wasn't morning. It would be hours before the police returned. And here I was, awake, with Lucas sleeping in my apartment. This wasn't the way I'd envisioned our first night together.

Everything seemed calm, quiet. What was happening down on the street? Was Graham Coates down there? Had the police found him? Had he tried to come back? It seemed ridiculous that he would risk returning and being seen when he'd threatened to kill me and police were patrolling the neighbourhood. For all he knew, I was somewhere else, or in the hospital, or dead. No. He didn't hit me hard enough to kill me, he made certain of that. He needed control. He had a plan, he'd said so himself.

I struggled into a sitting position, my head pounding with the movement. I pushed the covers back and dangled my legs over the side of the mattress. Marianne and Lucas hadn't stirred, hadn't heard me moving about.

I climbed to my feet and took a few steps towards the couch. 'Lucas?'

Instantly he shot into a sitting position, spinning around with wide eyes. 'You okay?'

'Sorry, you were asleep.'

'No, I'm awake,' he said, rubbing his hands down his face. He made room for me on the couch, moving the blanket aside. I caught a glimpse of his bare legs underneath as I sat. His jeans had been flung over the back of the couch, and I leaned against them, letting out a breath. 'How do you feel?' His hoarse whisper was surprisingly loud.

'My head hurts. And I'm sore here.' I pointed to my cheek.

He leaned over, studying my face in the dim light. 'You're bruised there, under your eye.'

'I don't remember.'

'Hmmm?'

'I don't remember him hitting me there. Just my head going back against the wall. And then the car. And I was on the ground and it was really cold.'

He didn't say anything.

'I tried to tell him that we didn't really know each other, to make him realise that he ...' I trailed off, suddenly unsure how to finish the thought.

'Let me check your head,' he said finally. I lowered my head, focusing on the toes of his socks poking out from the edge of the blanket. When his fingers began to slide through my hair, I fought not to close my eyes, instead staring hard at the floor, at his foot, his scratchy-looking woollen sock.

'Does this hurt?' he whispered.

'No,' I managed to breathe in reply. It didn't hurt. It didn't hurt at all. Not like when I'd tried to shampoo my hair in the shower. His fingers moved slowly and gently. When he reached the crown of my head, he withdrew his hand.

'You've got a big bump there.'

'Really?'

'Yeah, feel it.' He took my hand in his and guided my fingers. The lump was hot and hard, like half a golf ball sticking out. When I pressed, the pain ricocheted, shooting white-hot through my skull.

'That hurts,' I gasped. When he didn't answer, I sat up, meeting his eyes again in the darkness of the lounge room.

'I hate him,' he whispered, and his voice fractured.

I hesitated, unsure. 'I guess that's how he feels about you.'

'I didn't take his wife's head and slam it into a wall.'

'That's not what I meant.'

'I know.' He ran a hand over his eyes. He stared at the TV. On the screen, Niles sidled up behind Daphne and smelled her hair.

'Why did you stay?' I asked. There it was; the question that had been circling my mind that I wasn't sure I could ask out loud.

'I had to. It's my fault.'

'But should we even be here? Look what he did to me.

He could have killed me if he wanted to. I mean, he wants to. He was so calm at first, and he's been tracking me, like he's hunting me. He's going to try again.'

He faced me. 'Amanda, we're safe. The police are looking for him, and they're watching us too. He can't get in.'

I nodded, my stomach turning as I asked the next question. 'Why didn't you want Marianne to stay?'

Hurt flashed in his eyes. His mouth opened then closed. 'I never said that.' He paused, shaking his head. 'You really don't trust me.' He hadn't raised his voice at all, yet his words sliced into me. His house. The hot lounge room. Him asking about Marco, so angry. It all came back.

'No, it's not that. I just can't believe all this is happening. Yesterday everything was normal, and now … it doesn't feel real.'

'In a few hours it will all be over. They'll get him, they'll fix it. Everything will go back to normal.'

'I hope so.'

We fell silent. I studied him, not bothering to hide the fact I did so. He stared back, not saying anything. I could have asked him so much more – important things, but I couldn't form the words anymore. Maybe I was still tired. Maybe I did have some form of concussion. Had Lucas been watching me sleep? Had they heard from the police? What time were the cops coming back? So many questions, but I just sat looking at him. I felt as though I needed to register this moment, remember everything.

His hair hung to his shoulders, tucked messy behind his ears. He wore an old T-shirt, maybe the same one he had been wearing at his house. I couldn't remember. Frayed a bit at the collar, a pale blue or grey. It was hard to tell. He looked tired, but he looked sad, too. Worried. What he'd said, about Marco ... he was right. It was hard to trust Lucas, and not only because I hadn't known him for long, but because Marco had treated me like shit. *Two years ago.* God, where had that time gone? I'd wasted it; pretending I was okay about it. That I trusted men just fine, when clearly I didn't.

Lucas was studying me too. He wanted to know about Marco, I was sure, and probably about a lot of other things. I had to tell him. I had to trust him.

I ran my hand along his cheek, his jaw. He needed to shave, the stubble tickling my fingers. His hair was tangled, his neck warm. He smelled good. His lips were soft against mine. Lucas eased me onto his lap. I could feel him beneath me. All of him. Through my shirt, his thumb grazed my nipple. I groaned, and our kiss became urgent. His arms were tight across my back, our bodies crushed together. My head pounded, my back ached.

I pulled back. I didn't have to say anything. Lucas's smile was tinged with regret. He knew. I crawled back onto the couch next to him. Lucas wrapped us both in the blanket and we stared at the TV as *Frasier* ended and the credits began to roll.

*

Marianne left before the sun came up to buy produce for the restaurant at the markets. I hadn't been able to sleep after kissing Lucas; I'd gone back to bed and listened almost deliriously to Marianne's constant snoring, and Lucas's relentless turning. I guess he hadn't been able to sleep either.

With a hug from Marianne, and a promise to call her

with news, I dragged myself back to the couch where Lucas stirred underneath the blanket.

My head still ached, and Lucas was quiet. He seemed exhausted. We sat limply beside each other, and after a few minutes of silence, I fumbled for the TV remote and switched on the news.

'How do you feel?'

I shrugged. 'My head hurts.'

He cradled a warm palm over my ear and I nestled briefly against it.

'Want some coffee?'

I nodded, grateful. My body woke up, being so close to him. I was having a physical reaction to everything he was saying and doing, like him pulling on his jeans and the flash of his belly as he buttoned them up. I couldn't let myself get carried away. Not after what Graham Coates did last night. Not while I felt like this.

I frowned at the TV, trying to pay attention. Interest rates, the Aussie dollar. My head thumped harder. I rubbed at my temples.

Lucas was in the kitchen, lifting the bag of coffee beans out of the cupboard.

'Hey, are there any more of those pills?' I asked.

He glanced over his shoulder. 'I dunno. Is the pain that bad?' He abandoned the coffee and came to sit beside me. Before I knew what was happening, his hands were on my head, feeling for the bump on my scalp. 'It hasn't gone down that much. I'm taking you to the hospital.'

'No, really, I–'

A pounding on the door. I flew to my feet as Lucas sprang from the couch. I hovered behind him, my head thumping. I tried to hold it together with my hands.

'It's only seven thirty,' Lucas said, looking at his phone. 'Why are the police here so early?'

I didn't answer. Two words throbbed along with the pain in my skull. *Graham Coates.* It was illogical that he would knock on the door and announce himself … but pretty much everything about this situation defied logic.

'Who is it?' Lucas shouted.

'It's Constable Jason Richards, from Victoria Police. I was here last night.'

'Okay, hang on.' Lucas pointed to me. 'Get dressed.'

I yanked the curtain closed, pulled on jeans, a top, and Marianne's red leather jacket, and ran back to Lucas. He opened the door.

Constable Richards walked in alone, uniform crisp, looking like a soldier. Tall, broad-shouldered, with his hair cropped close. He was like T-1000. I couldn't imagine him being very easy to talk to.

'Did you find Coates?' Lucas asked.

'Unfortunately not. But we're still looking.' He smiled down at me, and I relaxed a little. 'Did you get some sleep, Amanda?'

I nodded.

'I don't get it,' Lucas said. 'Why can't you find him? You know his name and where he lives, right?'

'We're looking,' Constable Richards repeated. 'We think he may have left town. Either that or he's hiding in one of the listed properties. We didn't get to them all.'

'What?'

'He's a real estate agent.' He shot Lucas a look, as if he should have known that. 'He works for one of the biggest agencies in East Melbourne, and has quite a few vacant properties on the books.' He smiled at me again. 'We'll find him.'

'So you have to ask me more questions. Can I get you a cup of coffee or something?'

'Actually, Amanda, we'd like you to come into the station. We can take an official statement and discuss some options with you.'

'Okay.' I glanced at Lucas.

I slipped on my boots, fetched Oscar's scarf and my bag. We followed Constable Richards down the stairs and out to where a police car was parked at the kerb. The sun was lifting, bathing the street in a cool, milky light. A patch of red caught my eye on the footpath. Blood. *My* blood. I clenched my teeth and climbed into the back seat of the police car. Doors slammed. Lucas sat next to me, briefly squeezing my fingers.

Constable Richards pulled out of my street, and I nestled into the seat.

We crawled along Sydney Road, and the slow pace of traffic and thrum of morning activity lulled me into a relaxed state, easing the ache in my head. It was the familiarity – people on their way to work, or school, or wherever they spent their day. Cars, trams, and bikes and pedestrians all shuffling along, all sharing the road. Despite last night's events, everything was exactly the same once I stepped outside. I lowered myself a little, moving my head to the side so I could rest it back without touching the tender area. Lucas turned to face me and we exchanged a smile. The light through the windows had lit up his face, paling his eyelashes, highlighting the creases around his eyes. I remembered then the night at Alberto's, when the lights behind the bar had made his shirt glow bright white. The light played on him in a way I'd never noticed with anyone else before.

'You right?' he whispered. He was smiling, his eyes crinkling, watching me watch him.

'I will be soon.'

'Let me take you to the doctor later.'

I nodded. I didn't know what to do about work, but I would have to call them at some point to tell them I wouldn't be in today. Later, when hopefully they'd found the bastard and I could forget about all of this.

Where had Coates gone after he'd left me in the gutter? Was he feeling the fear and the pressure of being watched as the police closed in on him? I hoped so. Maybe then he'd realise how I'd been feeling. But how much time could the police dedicate to finding him anyway, and how hard would they look? They'd give up sooner or later, wouldn't they?

Constable Richards whipped a phone from his pocket as it vibrated. He glanced at the screen and said over his shoulder, 'We have to make a quick stop first. Will only take a second.'

Lucas leaned forward. 'Are you kidding me? Shouldn't we get this sorted?'

'It can't be helped, Mr Williams,' he answered, without turning.

'But–'

'Please sit back in your seat, Mr Williams.'

Lucas sat back and sighed. 'I don't believe this.'

Constable Richards kept driving without another word. I reached across the seat for Lucas and gripped his hand. I was annoyed too, but I needed to keep him calm. He rubbed my knuckles with his fingertips and I watched the slow movement as it brought me gently back into that same relaxed state. Maybe the drugs had lingered after all. My mouth slackened and my eyelids grew heavy until I could barely keep my eyes open. I could feel his gaze on me for what felt like a long time, and I didn't mind at all.

'Are you okay?'

I nodded myself back to reality.

'Does your head still hurt?'

'Yeah,' I murmured. When his eyes narrowed, I added, 'but not as bad.'

'We really need to talk to a doctor. We could go where you work, right?'

'Yeah, we'll go and see Dr Kim.'

'You got a lot of sleep last night, so I really think you should get checked out again for concussion.'

I smiled. 'I'm okay. It'll pass. Hey, did you watch me sleep last night?'

He blinked. 'What?'

'If you were worried about me and my head, did you check on me while I was asleep?'

He ran his fingers across my knuckles again. His palm had become sweaty in mine, or maybe it was my hand that had. 'I did,' he said finally with a soft laugh. 'We both did.'

I grinned back. 'I'd taken those painkillers, so I wouldn't know what you did last night.'

He cocked his head with a smile. 'I'm not the one you need to be worried about, you know.'

'I know.' Remembering Constable Richards, I glanced over, and met his eyes in the rear view mirror. My stomach flipped; I didn't want him listening. I brought my hand back into my lap and looked out the window. I spotted a sign for the Cabrini Hospital and frowned. Constable Richards turned the car into a residential street. It was the upper-class, big shady tree kind of street with large houses and tall iron gates.

I glanced at Lucas. He held my gaze.

The car came to a stop in a driveway partly shielded by tall hedges. The house behind was a neat place, protected from the neighbours by a stone wall. My eyes swept over the clipped strip of grass, sparkling with frost under the morning sun. Punctuating the lawn was a sign that had been hammered into the earth: *For Sale*.

'Where are we?' Lucas demanded, unbuckling his seat belt.

Constable Richards didn't say anything. He didn't turn, he didn't move.

I unbuckled my own seat belt, my stomach clenched tight. Something wasn't right here. I was watching Lucas reach for his door handle when a movement from the house caught my eye.

Graham Coates.

Chapter 9

As Graham Coates approached the police car, Constable Richards jumped from behind the wheel. Moving quickly, he opened the back door and dove in on top of Lucas, straddled him, and before I knew what was happening, began to punch him in the face. Lucas thrashed forward, trying to force him off, but he wasn't quick enough. Richards punched him again, and Lucas fell back against the seat.

'Get her out, get her out!' Richards screamed.

I couldn't move.

Coates opened my door.

Cold air slapped my face, and then his hands were on me. I tried to yell, but my voice betrayed me again. He hauled me to my feet, grabbed my arms. My belly pressed against the cold metal of the car.

Lucas. He was dragged out of the seat, his hair hanging over his face. His body was limp, and I couldn't see his expression. Constable Richards tossed him over his shoulder, biceps bulging, and began to walk towards the house.

I didn't fight; I didn't resist. Coates led me quickly along a smooth path, up steps that shone with morning dew. I passed through the enormous door and into a large open room with polished boards and floor-to-ceiling windows. The house was vacant. No furniture or art on the walls. The door thumped closed behind us. Richards dropped Lucas to the floor and strode from the room towards a modern kitchen mostly obscured behind sliding doors.

Lucas was on his side with his back to me. I tried to wrench myself free from Coates. His face was pale and empty, but he let go. I ran to Lucas and fell to my knees. At my touch, Lucas rolled onto his back. I leaned over him.

'Did he hit you?' he whispered, his teeth red with blood.

'No.' I scooped my hands under him and helped him sit up. 'How are we going to get out of here?'

'You're not,' Coates said, and walked over to us. 'Now if you can help Lucas up, please, I'd like to get you away from all these windows.'

I bit my lip as tears threatened. 'But we didn't do anything.'

His face remained unchanged. 'Come on, get him up.'

I stared at Coates; I had to figure out how to get through to him. Soon. Time wasn't on our side. Coates looked dishevelled, in ripped jeans and a plain T shirt. He looked *regular*.

'Come on,' he snapped, impatient.

Lucas and I grasped hands. I stood, pulling him with me.

'Good, now through that door there.'

We walked through a doorway and into a dark, narrow hall.

'Up to the end.'

We walked in what felt like slow motion, our feet silent on the plush grey carpet. I was walking almost certainly to my death, with Coates only a couple of paces behind.

This man wanted to kill me. Like prisoners herded into the last room we would ever see, were these our last moments together? I wondered what the prisoners felt before they were beheaded by terrorists, knowing they were about to die but unable to stop it. My brain couldn't process what was happening.

Numb. I felt numb.

At the end of the hall, an empty, carpeted room. A bedroom once, I guessed. A blind covered the window, casting it in darkness. We stood in the centre of the room, Coates opposite. Lucas was pale, and his hair plastered over his face in such a way that I couldn't see his eyes.

I needed to. I needed to know if he had any fight in him, or if he'd given up. I knew the longer we were in this house, the harder it would be to get away, and I couldn't do it by myself. I'd managed to fight off Coates last night, but I'd needed help. This morning, my head was pounding from being knocked around, and Constable Richards was in the house somewhere too. A police officer, for fuck's sake. Someone we should have been able to trust.

Richards came into the room and handed Coates a roll of silver duct tape. My stomach lurched.

'Amanda, sit on the floor please.'

I didn't move, but in my head was screaming.

'You can't,' Lucas said.

'Oh, I can't? If I have to do this to show you what you've done to me, then that's what I'll do,' Coates shouted, spit flying as he shook the roll of tape. 'You can't wipe it from your memory and go on like nothing's happened!'

'You think that's what I've done?' Lucas yelled back. 'I

think about that accident every single fucking day!'

'Do you? Do you?' Coates screamed. He was losing control. All the calm and restraint was gone. 'What did you lose? Tell me, what the fuck did you lose that day?'

Constable Richards touched Coates's arm, but he wrenched it away.

'Keep it down,' Richards pleaded. 'Let's just get this over with.' His eyes darted between us, his fingers twitching.

My heart raced. Maybe this was my shot – Coates was angry, Richards nervous. Maybe–

I lunged at Coates, pushing him as hard as I could.

Then I ran.

Shouting erupted in the room behind me, thumping against the walls. I kept going, reaching the hallway door, when rough arms gripped my waist. Frantically I kicked my legs. I was being dragged backwards, my head against someone's chest. In the darkness of the empty bedroom, I was thrown to the floor. My head slammed against the wall as I hit the carpet.

I rolled over in time to see Coates drive his knee into Lucas's belly, and the sound as the rush of air escaped made me scream. I screamed as loud as I could, tearing up the surface of my throat, begging for someone to hear, or for someone out on the street to notice the police car in the driveway and wonder what was going on. But why would anyone question noise, or screaming, when a police car was already here? Police were supposed to sort things out, to get rid of the bad and protect the neighbourhood.

No one would come to investigate. Lucas and I were going to die in this empty house, in this strange neighbourhood.

Richards crouched in front of me and wrapped a hand

around my throat. My scream melted away as he applied pressure. With his other hand, he held a finger in front of his mouth. *Shhh.*

Lucas hit the floor with a thud.

Coates breathed heavily, hands on hips. He glanced at me. 'I *am* sorry about all this.'

Richards moved away, and I swallowed. I could still feel his hand on my throat. It felt raw, the woollen scarf irritating the skin. I coughed, clearing my throat. 'How do you think you're going to get away with this?' I whispered.

Coates shook his head. 'I'm not expecting to. And I don't care. I died in that accident too.'

I hung my head. I couldn't look at him anymore. I wouldn't be able to change his mind.

He was going to kill us.

'I know this isn't your fault. I really *am* sorry, Amanda,' he said softly. He knelt in front of me, so close that I could feel his breath against my skin. He pressed my hands together, holding them between his. He squeezed them for a moment, and his wedding band bit into my flesh.

He reached for the roll of tape and began to wind it tightly around my wrists. Instantly blood pounded in my fingers. The tape was too tight. But what did that matter? I looked past him, at the dark shape of Lucas on the carpet.

Unmoving.

Coates lifted me in his arms, leaning me against the wall and drawing my legs out towards him. I began to kick, but then Richards stepped out from the doorway. I stopped, managing to stifle a sob. I lowered my head, closing my eyes as Coates began to tape my ankles together. When I eventually looked up, both Coates and Richards had left the room.

*

I nudged Lucas with my feet. He was still sprawled face down on the carpet, unmoving. In the dark, I couldn't tell if he was breathing. I pressed my lips together, refusing to scream. If I did, they would return and wouldn't be so patient. They'd kill me. Eventually. They would wait. Until Lucas woke.

I sighed. For Lucas to suffer, I had to die first.

I swallowed. My throat was on fire. Richards could have ended it, choked me until it was over. But despite the uniform, Richards wasn't in charge. This was all Coates – he'd probably been dreaming of it for months; how to get back at the man who had taken his wife. Stalking Lucas, waiting for him to grow close to someone. Waiting for his chance. Part of me wanted to feel sorry for Coates, and last night after I'd spoken to Lucas, I had. Briefly. Maybe Lucas had caused the accident. Maybe it really was his fault. Maybe he'd been drinking, or speeding, or had fallen asleep at the wheel. Maybe Coates was just a husband who couldn't live without his wife.

Voices floated to me from another area of the house, but they were soft, indistinguishable. The house had looked big from the outside. Surely Richards wasn't going to help Coates kill us and then head back into the station as if it was a normal work day. Maybe he wasn't a cop at all. Maybe it was all fake – the car, the uniform. Maybe the woman at my apartment last night hadn't been real either.

My mind wandered. Time ticked slowly by, and my

delirium built. How long were they going to leave me here? Why wasn't Lucas waking up?

It didn't really matter anyway. This house was going to become the scene of a murder-suicide. The house would never sell if people knew the truth.

I almost laughed. *Like it mattered.* But it made sense. The house's history would be tainted forever. People would look away when they passed it on the street, or worse, gossip and speculate about what we'd done to deserve such a fate. Children would tell stories and frighten each other, peeking through the windows and pointing out the possible blood stains. The police would shrug, case closed.

But we'd done the right thing, hadn't we? We had reported Coates and what he'd done, passing on as much information as we could – the sightings at the restaurant and my place, and the attack last night.

But we'd reported all of this to Constable Richards. So maybe there was no record at all.

The voices rose in pitch, and now I could identify Coates and Richards. They both sounded agitated; straining my ears, I tried desperately to pick out particular words.

'You know why I'm doing this!' Richards.

'For fuck's sake,' Coates barked back.

Lucas stirred. His leg moved then his arm twitched. I nudged him again, harder this time. He lifted his head, blinking rapidly as he looked at me. He crawled slowly on his belly, silent on the thick carpet. He tugged at the tape on my wrists, and we both winced at the sound of it ripping free.

'I've been saying, man, cut the fucking theatrics and get a gun.'

'Look, you've got your money. You can go.'

Lucas rested on his knees a moment, my bound hands in his. He grimaced; his face shadowy in the dark room. Blood? It was hard to tell.

He tried once again, picking at the tape. Centimetre by centimetre he unwound it, using the conversation outside to cover the ripping sound.

'You didn't even tie him up–'

'He's out cold.'

Bundling up the sticky wads of tape, Lucas started on my ankles. I bit my lip and prayed for Coates and Richards to keep talking. Once free, Lucas held my hand and we inched silently from the room, down the hallway, the thick carpet cushioning our steps.

Leaning against the wall, we listened.

'You better take care of this. You've fucked it up once before.'

'I can. I will.'

'Yeah, well, they've seen my face, you know? They know who I am. I've sorted it as best I can, and–'

'That was your choice–'

'My choice? You didn't give me much choice. And my job is on the line here.'

'All right, all right, keep your fucking voice down. I'm ending this today.'

'Right, well, don't fuck it up this time. My involvement ends here.'

'Thanks, Jason.'

'Don't fucking thank me.'

Distant footsteps. A door slamming.

Muttered curses from Coates. 'Fuck, fuck, fuck.'

I gripped Lucas's hand.

We had to make a run for it.

Coates was alone, with no gun, but any minute he could come back and find us in the hallway.

We had to move now.

Lucas led the way through the doorway and into the large empty room we'd first entered. Polished floors, gleaming windows ... no Coates.

Lucas stared at me. His eyes were hard, his mouth set.

He nodded.

I nodded back.

I focused on the front door, a heavy, bright-red wooden thing. It would be impossible to get through it silently, or quickly. We stepped closer, our feet quiet. Marianne always commented how loud my boots were, how the sound preceded my arrival. Not today. My life depended on it.

I pushed the thought of her out of my mind. I couldn't think of her now.

Focus.

We were halfway across the room when Coates walked in.

We froze.

He froze.

Then he charged.

Lucas pushed me toward the door as Coates caught him, yanking him backwards.

I grabbed at the door handle, but stopped and glanced over my shoulder.

Lucas was on top of Coates, slamming his head into the floorboards. Coates grabbed at Lucas's neck; he shrugged the man's hands off. Lucas was winning.

But with a roar, Coates threw Lucas from him.

Blood ran down the side of Coates's face as he glared at me.

Lucas pushed to his feet as Coates thundered towards me.

I tugged at the door handle, desperate.

Coates yanked me back and threw me to the floor.

Coates screamed.

Lucas screamed.

Lucas hauled me to my feet; swung me around.

We fell in slow-motion.

We passed through the window pane.

Light caught the fragments of glass as they showered down like diamonds. The green blur of grass rushed up at us. I landed hard on top of Lucas, our bodies slamming together amongst huge shards of glass. My ears were ringing. Blood. But who was bleeding?

Lucas was making so much noise ... No. Coates ran at us, his shoes crunching on broken glass.

Lucas rolled me out of the minefield and I pushed myself up.

'Run,' Lucas yelled. He struggled to his feet, the glass sliding off him and tinkling to the ground as he stood.

Head spinning, pounding, I raced across the front yard, bypassed a shrub, and pelted over the driveway. The police car was gone. I expected neighbours to be peering out of their houses, alarmed by the noise, but the street was empty.

I shot a glance over my shoulder; Lucas was behind me.

'Run,' he shouted again, before spitting a mouthful of blood onto the footpath.

I charged into the street, not knowing where I was going.

Lucas appeared beside me, grabbing my hand as we ran. His legs were longer, and despite his right leg dragging, he was fast. I wanted to stop and catch my breath, but I knew at any second Coates could appear behind us. Somehow we'd made it out of the house. I couldn't stop. He must have had a car at the house, or waiting nearby.

Oh, fuck.

I pushed on.

We crossed the intersection, pounding down the pavement and on to the next block. The houses were smaller here, older.

Lucas slowed. 'We have to get some help,' he gasped. 'If Coates has a car, we're fucked.'

I followed him up a nearby driveway. We knocked on the door of a neat weatherboard cottage.

'Come on,' Lucas murmured, shuffling his feet on the *Welcome* doormat. He pounded his fist against the door again. Nothing. We ran to the house next door. In the driveway, a white commodore sat with its doors and boot wide open. A few shopping bags waited to be unloaded from the back. The door to the house was open too, voices carrying outside. I started to run towards the house when Lucas yanked me back. He glanced at the car. The keys were still in the ignition, glinting in the sun.

I gaped at him. 'No.'

'We don't have time,' Lucas hissed.

For the first time since we'd left the house, I looked at him properly. He had blood on his face and in his hair. His jacket was torn and streaked with blood, his lip split. His body leaned to the left, with no weight on his right foot.

We had to get out of here.

I crawled into the passenger seat. Lucas lowered the boot then slid behind the wheel. When he started the engine, bass guitar throbbed from the stereo speakers. Both of us instantly slammed a hand against the power button. I braced myself, waiting for the people in the house to run outside, shouting. Lucas rammed the car into reverse and it shot out onto the road. No one ran out, no one noticed. For a quiet neighbourhood, these people were totally unfazed by noise.

I leaned back, buckling my seat belt, and tried to catch my breath. Lucas sped through the unfamiliar neighbourhood, and no matter how many intersections we passed through, I couldn't orient myself. 'Do you know where we are?'

He shook his head. 'Can you see him?'

I twisted around to look through the back windscreen. There were no cars behind us at all, and no black BMW. 'No. There's no one.'

Lucas swung the car onto a busy road. A red traffic light loomed ahead.

'Fuck.'

Slowing the car, we waited as pedestrians crossed; a group of girls in school uniform, a woman with a pram. The girls cackled maniacally in that teenage way that begged attention, while the mother panicked, trying to veer the pram around them.

'Where are we going?'

'I don't know,' he snapped, running a hand over his face. 'Sorry. I don't know.'

'We have to go to the police.'

He shot me a look. 'We did. Last night.'

I pressed a hand against my stomach. The light flicked green and Lucas surged through the crossing, changing lanes.

'I'll get on the freeway,' he said. 'He won't be able to stop us.'

'Okay.' A lump rose in my aching throat, acid reaching my back teeth. 'He's got my bag.'

Lucas glanced across at me.

'It was in the police car. I don't know where it went.' I struggled for a breath, my mouth gaping. 'I need my phone. I need to call Marianne or something. We have to call someone.'

'As soon as we can stop, we'll figure out what to do.'

Lucas took the exit. The ramp swept us around and spat us out onto the freeway. Rubbing my hands over my jeans, I willed myself to calm down. My stomach rolled. I felt unclean. My hands were dirty. I examined them, turning them over. Blood caked between several of my fingers and under my nails. I wound down the window and gulped in air that stunk of exhaust fumes.

'Amanda?'

'I think I'm going to be sick.'

'I can't stop here.' His hand reached for mine. 'Hang on a little bit.'

Acid and panic rose from my empty stomach. I gasped helplessly for air. My throat started to close, and my eyes stung with tears. The panic was pulling me under.

'Oh my God. How did we get out of there? How did we do that? We nearly died,' I cried, squeezing my eyes shut.

Lucas gripped my fingers. 'Stay calm.'

I shook my head. 'And what happens when these people report their car stolen?' I shouted over the wind churning through the car.

'That's the least of our worries.'

'We stole their car.'

'We had no choice.' He let go of my hand. He looked in the mirrors, his head moving all the time. 'As soon as we can stop, we'll call someone.'

I didn't answer. He was right. We needed to get some distance.

Where the hell was Coates?

Chapter 10

We left the city behind.

The scenery flashed past in a blur until Lucas pointed to the side of the road. An exit ramp led to what looked like a cluster of shops with a petrol station, cafes and a supermarket.

'We should stop and work out what to do,' he said. 'Are you hungry?'

The last time I'd eaten had been the cannoli at the cafe yesterday afternoon, but I wasn't hungry. My stomach churned at the thought of putting anything else in it. My throat was dry and sore though. I needed water.

'Thirsty,' I answered.

Lucas drove into the massive car park. We passed signs for KFC and McDonalds, an ATM, a supermarket. The parking spaces were mostly full but we found an empty spot far from the entrance and facing the road. Cars whizzed by in the distance in streaks of colour. Was Coates one of them? It wouldn't be possible for him to find us this far out of the city ... would it?

I climbed out of the car and leaned against it. Lucas was doing the same thing on the other side, pale-faced, eyes closed. When I touched him, he whispered, 'My knee. It's my knee.' He slapped his hand hard against the top of his thigh, and let out a low groan. 'I'm not supposed to run.'

'Shit,' I breathed. 'You probably shouldn't be driving either.'

He took a deep breath. 'I haven't ... since the accident.' He shook his head. 'You know what ... you should look in the boot. There might be some food.' He passed me the keys and I went to the back of the car. Two white plastic bags sat in there. A pang of guilt echoed in my belly as I rifled through them. In one, I found toilet paper, a box of tissues and fly spray. In the other was a *New Idea* magazine, three sachets of microwave soup, lip balm and shampoo. I held up the soup and he sighed. 'That's it? Perfect.'

'Let's go inside, get something to eat and drink.' I glanced over my shoulder. It was busy in there, and I didn't want attention. But we needed to sit down and work out what to do.

'We'll have to clean up first.' Lucas was still covered in dried blood, his hair matted. He was right. I desperately wanted to wash my hands.

We walked slowly towards the zebra crossing, Lucas dragging his leg behind him. As the sliding doors parted, we passed a pot-bellied man. 'Whoa, you okay, mate?'

'Yeah, thanks,' Lucas called back, waving him away.

Inside, counters surrounded a huge seating area. To the left, a supermarket led through to a petrol station. To the right, KFC sat alongside McDonald's, a coffee counter, and a sandwich shop. Directly in front, a doorway led to the toilets.

'We'll meet back here and get something to eat,' Lucas said.

I nodded and started down the long tiled corridor to the Ladies'. Public toilets were always the same; shielded from the public for sanitary reasons, and yet, created the perfect buffer zone for rapists to strike. I'd never felt safe using them alone, and today was no different. Only the predator wasn't a stranger whose face was blurred on the TV news, but Graham Coates. If I could turn back the clock and get Lucas out of Alberto's, so we never met, so I didn't even know he existed, would I? If I could promise Coates that if he left me alone I would never see Lucas again ... I would move forward without looking back and forget this whole thing. Wouldn't I? But I wasn't a monster. I was well aware of my shortcomings and my lack of trust towards others, especially men, but I wasn't a monster. I wouldn't leave Lucas to hobble through this shit by himself.

The bathroom light was fluorescent and stark. I scanned the gaps under the cubicle doors for feet, and satisfied I was alone, went to a sink and turned on the tap. First, I scrubbed at my hands with antibacterial soap, rubbing away all traces of blood. Then I examined my face in the mirror. Beneath the scarf, my throat was blotched with pink, where Constable Richards had grabbed and squeezed, and the bruise underneath my eye had darkened. My nose still looked swollen, and my eyes looked tired, but I didn't look half as battered as Lucas. A few scratches marked the left side of my face, the side that Lucas hadn't been able to completely protect from the window. I touched one on my cheek and winced. I leaned in as close as I could to the mirror, and used my nails to pick out a splinter of glass.

The door to the bathroom swung open, slamming against the tiled wall. I spun around, my pulse screaming. A woman with grey hair piled up on top of her head jumped, clutching a hand to her ample breast. 'My goodness, I'm sorry. You scared me.'

I laughed; a breathless, relieved sound. 'I'm sorry.'

*

Lucas was waiting for me outside. He'd done the same thing and scrubbed himself free of blood, but in his case it didn't make him look much better, just made his injuries all the more visible. His bottom lip was split right down the middle, and his nose was cut underneath one nostril. The whole left side of his face was swollen, looking almost as if he'd been attacked by a swarm of bees.

'Ready?' he asked, tucking a chunk of wet hair behind his ear.

We found the most inconspicuous table we could, partially hidden behind a potted fern. People were all around us though: several older couples, a young family, a group of teenage boys, and a dozen or so solitary men who looked like truck drivers.

Lucas sat awkwardly with a grunt.

I sat opposite. 'So what are we gonna do?'

'I don't know,' he answered. 'We should call the police, but now I don't know about that.'

'Please tell me you have your phone.'

The woman from the bathroom sat at the next table, caught my eye and smiled. I smiled back.

Lucas slid his phone out of his pocket and placed it on the table between us. 'We could go to Doug's. Remember I told you about him?'

'Your neighbour?'

'Yeah. He was a cop. He's retired now. But he'll know what to do.'

I nodded eagerly. 'Let's do that. We need someone we can trust.'

'Okay. Call Marianne first, and tell her to warn Cam. Then I'll call Doug and tell him we're coming.'

I picked up his phone, found Marianne's number in his contact list, and hit 'call'.

'Lucas?'

My throat tightened when I heard her voice. This morning, I thought I was about to lose her for good, and maybe I still would. 'No it's me.'

'Amanda, what's wrong?' The tone of her voice changed. With only the three words I'd spoken, she knew.

'We're in trouble.'

'What do you mean? They haven't found him? Are they at your apartment right now? What's going on? Tell me.'

She fired the questions so fast, I immediately forgot them. I swallowed. 'Constable Richards came over this morning. But he took us to a house and Graham Coates was there.' A heavy silence filled my ear. I braced myself for a profanity-laden explosion of rage, but none came. I continued. 'We got away and we ran, but Lucas is pretty hurt, so we're going to Doug's and we have to warn you and Cam too, so you have to tell Cam that we're going to Doug's–'

Lucas held up a hand. *Slow down.* I dragged in a breath.

'What?' Marianne was asking. 'Who's Doug? What?'

I told her again, slower this time. Eventually, she asked to speak to Lucas. I passed him the phone, and although I couldn't hear what she was saying, I could figure it out by watching Lucas's expression.

'I promise,' Lucas said. He said it twice more before disconnecting the call. Today there were no comments or jokes about her intensity. And today I wanted nothing more than to be reassured by her – to be at Alberto's prepping in the kitchen and hanging out at the bar.

Lucas handed me his wallet. 'Do you mind getting some food while I ring Doug?'

I went to the sandwich counter, selecting a couple from the fridge that looked fresh. I grabbed two bottles of water and queued to pay.

'Are you all right?' the woman behind the counter asked. She was leaning across, peering into my face.

I drew back. 'Yes, I'm fine.'

'Are you sure?'

'Yes, thank you. Had a little accident, but I'm fine, really.' I drew a fifty out of the wallet and thrust it towards her. She took it with a frown, and handed over my change.

I carried the food to the table. Lucas was still on the phone so I headed over to the coffee counter and ordered two lattes. By the time they were ready, Lucas had hung up and was tapping his fingertips on the tabletop.

'So what did Doug say? Are we meeting him at a police station somewhere or what?' I unscrewed a bottle of water and took a long drink, the cool water soothing my raw throat. Instantly I felt a little better.

'No, he said to come to his place. He's calling his friend David, who he used to work with. He said we can stay with him until this is sorted. He also said we shouldn't stay on the road too long, so as soon as we eat we'll get going. It takes a few hours to get there.'

'Get where?' I unwrapped an egg and lettuce sandwich and bit into it.

He took a sip of his coffee. 'To Doug's.'

I frowned at him. 'Where does he live?'

'About three hours away at Hanley. I didn't mention that?'

'No.' I put down my sandwich.

'He moved there after he retired.'

'I don't think we should drive that far. Shouldn't we go back into the city?'

'There's no one else I can think of who can help figure this out. I mean, we can find the closest police station and take our chances.' He gave a helpless shrug. 'But I thought we were safe last night, and this morning when he came back I thought we were safe. They said they were patrolling your street, and looking for him, but now I don't know. If Richards is involved in this, then there could be others.' He slapped a hand on the table top. 'Who do we trust now?'

I replayed last night, after I'd woken and found Lucas on my couch. *Frasier* and the blanket and the kiss and his fingers brushing my breasts. It seemed so long ago that I'd sat on his lap and felt him underneath me, and it was so irrelevant now. One thing was certain – we should never have stayed there. We should have gone to Marianne's, or I should have spent the night in the hospital. I'd been right after all; we had been vulnerable, only I hadn't expected things to turn out the way they had.

Lucas was watching me carefully. 'What are you thinking? Will you come with me?'

He'd saved my life this morning. He'd held my hand and tried to protect me from Richards and Coates. He'd done everything he could to get us out of this mess. I had to trust him. 'Yeah, I'll go with you.'

Chapter 11

I drove the stolen car, following Lucas's directions. It didn't take long for small towns to pop up like blisters on the landscape ahead. The city was well and truly behind us. The concrete expanse of freeway gave way to a country highway, and paddocks, cows, and trees.

Lucas had pushed the passenger seat all the way back and his right leg was stretched out. His left leg bounced rapidly, relentlessly. He twisted from side to side, resting on one shoulder, then the other. The mask of pain was back on his face again.

'You're going to have to see a doctor or something,' I said.

'I can't think about that right now.'

I drove carefully, sticking to the speed limit with my eyes trained on the rear view mirror, mentally recording the scenery. The traffic was steady. The sun had come out. It was almost midday, and I was exhausted. My head pounding, my eyes felt like sandpaper. I longed to curl up in my bed and forget about all of this. A couple more of those painkillers wouldn't hurt, either.

'I was thinking about last night,' I found myself saying. 'Everything we talked about, you know ... on the couch.'

He smiled. 'Yeah.'

'It seems like so long ago, doesn't it?'

He rested his head back and sighed.

An hour later, we stopped to fill up at a service station. The tank wasn't empty but Lucas wanted to get out of the car to stretch his legs. The station was isolated – two lonely bowsers surrounded by paddocks. Its yellow sign was a beacon against the sweep of dry grass, but we were the only people there. While Lucas filled the tank, I paced the small asphalted area. The air stunk of manure. I walked to the closest fence, bordering a paddock filled with cows. Through the flimsy wire, a sea of tall grass swayed in the breeze, and the cows turned their heads, lazy eyes uninterested.

We drove on. Lucas had been sending text messages to Cam and Marianne, updating them on our progress, and asking if they'd heard anything. They knew I didn't have my bag, and I wondered if Coates had tried to access my phone. The thought of my leather bag in his hands made me sick. The messages beeped back and forth. Marianne and Cam hadn't heard anything, and they'd promised to wait until we reached Doug's before calling anyone else for help. I imagined Marianne's impatience, her insistence.

I felt far away. Isolated.

The road stretched on, a boring black ribbon punctuated by absolutely nothing. I clenched my hands around the steering wheel and tried not to plant my foot. This was taking forever. Now that we had a plan, I was impatient for Doug to start sorting this out. I wanted to go home. I wanted this over.

I was starting to feel delirious by the relentless swinging of the tree-shaped air freshener over the rear view mirror. As far as I could tell, the freshness of it had run out a while ago. The smell in the car was stale and unclean. Food wrappers littered the floor of the back seat and dust peppered the dashboard. The owners would have reported the theft by now, I realised. I pushed away the thought.

The paddocks gave way to scrubby trees that became thicker the farther we drove. It was obvious Lucas was becoming weaker as time wore on, and I didn't know what that meant. How hurt was he, exactly? I'd skipped the first aid course when offered at the clinic, and now I really wished I'd taken it. I did whatever I could to stem the flow of frantic thoughts ricocheting against the tender sides of my head, trying instead to concentrate on our destination. I was banking on Doug, former cop – a man I'd never met – to know exactly what to do to fix this.

Lucas pointed. 'There's the water. We're nearly there.'

I followed his finger; where a triangle of ocean was visible through the trees. Even from this distance it looked dark, choppy, and terrifying.

'Doug lives at the beach?'

'Yeah, in an old holiday house where we used to stay. I spent a lot of time here growing up. He taught me how to surf and everything. Then he moved here for good after he retired.'

'Can you see the water from his house?' I asked, keeping the tremor from my voice.

'Yeah, he has a great view.'

I navigated the winding road until Lucas told me to turn right. It was practically bush; trees so thick I couldn't see through the branches. I could hear the sweet music of birds, even though the windows were rolled up. A sign ahead warned of gravel, so I slowed the car. We bumped onto an unsealed road, where patches of trees had been cleared to make way for houses. We passed wooden fences that had mailboxes on them made out of barrels, and dusty 4WD vehicles in the driveways. Houses were set back from the road with verandas and tin rooves, and had the occasional horse flicking its tail in the breeze.

Lucas pointed again. 'Keep going up there.'

The road grew steeper. Houses became fewer, the blocks larger. Gates had signs on them, with painted names for the property like "Tea Tree Lane", and "Sea Mist Views". I smiled to myself. They couldn't come up with anything better than that?

We came to a T-junction and I turned left when Lucas pointed. 'See that green fence? Turn in there.'

I drove towards the faded fence palings. I couldn't see houses anymore, only the occasional gap where the trees parted unceremoniously for a dusty gravel track. I steered the car into the narrow driveway. On the corner post, a rusty mailbox read "Cooper", painted in flaking black letters above the number eleven.

The driveway was long and steep. It took several minutes before we reached the crest of the hill and a house became visible. As the car crept closer towards Doug's house, we passed a huge shed on the left with a couple of cars half-hidden under tarps. The house sat in a clearing, a peeling weatherboard place with a blue tin roof and a veranda in a rickety wooden rectangle out the front. The gravel driveway led to the front door, turning in a half circle around a flowerless garden.

I hadn't even turned off the ignition when the front door swung open and a man swaggered outside. Short and mostly bald, with a big belly hanging over his pants, he looked about seventy. A yellow Lab followed him down the steps, wagging its tail. Lucas was climbing out of the car already so I couldn't ask him, *is that really Doug?*

Lucas hobbled towards Doug and the men embraced. Doug held Lucas's face tenderly in both hands and stared up into it with a sense of fatherly love so strong it radiated off him. I felt a bit uncomfortable, as if I was intruding on a personal moment. I'd never had that closeness with my own father, let alone my mother. As soon as I opened the car door, I heard the hiss of the ocean in the distance. I stepped out and the chilly air kissed my cheeks with mist. I shivered, lingering behind Lucas as he and Doug exchanged murmured conversation, until Doug caught my eye.

'This is Amanda Ray.' Lucas beckoned me over. 'Doug Cooper.'

Doug wrapped his arms around me, squeezing me against his chest. His rough hands patted my back between the shoulder blades and hesitantly, I reached my own hands around him.

'Pleasure. Come inside, it's cold.' He thumped across the veranda and held the door open for us. 'And this is Bessie,' he smiled, nodding at the dog waddling through the doorway.

Inside, I was drawn immediately to the roaring fire in the hearth. The lounge room was cosy warm, with a mantelpiece full of framed photos and a patchy multi-coloured rug covering the threadbare carpet. The fire crackled as I thawed in front of it, scanning the photos in their tarnished frames.

There were many of Lucas and several looked quite recent. Still with his long hair, he stood with Cam on the beach, bare-chested and tanned and holding a surfboard. In another, he was drinking from a giant mug of beer. In another, he had an arm wrapped around someone who looked eerily similar, only his mate had short hair. His brother, I realised. Ben. Two boys in their school uniforms sat side by side, their collars crisp and clean, their blue eyes shining out from under a mop of white-blonde hair. One looked slightly older, sat taller. It must have been Lucas – Lucas as a schoolboy. My heart leapt.

'Nah, it doesn't make any difference. They told me not to run on it,' Lucas was saying. 'I'll be right. It doesn't matter. We just need you to help us sort this stuff out with Graham Coates.'

'Of course it matters.' Doug clapped a hand over his shoulder. 'You need to look after that knee or else they might not be able to fix it.'

'I'd rather keep my life and have a fucked-up knee–'

'Watch your language,' Doug growled. I suppressed a smile and turned back to the pictures. A woman with sleek red hair dominated most of the frames. She was with Doug in some of them – a younger Doug who had more hair. She looked younger than him, but not young enough to be a daughter. I would have to ask Lucas about her.

'Amanda, are you hungry? I've made us a late lunch.' Doug beckoned me to follow him through the doorway, and I walked into the kitchen. A table overflowing with food sat in the middle of the room. Sandwiches piled high on a platter, a plate of choc chip cookies, a bowl of fresh fruit, and a teapot covered with a crocheted cosy and sitting on a heatproof mat. Three places were set with plates, a tea cup and saucer, and a serviette folded into a triangle.

Wow. While we raced up here in a stolen car, Doug had been fussing around setting the table and folding serviettes in a triangle? I wasn't sure what I expected, but it certainly wasn't this.

Lucas limped up next to me and I raised my eyebrows at him. He smiled.

Doug was busy filling the teapot with boiling water. He gestured to a jug of milk and I nodded, pulling out a chair.

'Okay, so what should we do? You know, it's not just Coates, it's this cop,' Lucas began, biting into a sandwich. I stared at the pile of them, remembering the one I'd eaten only a few hours earlier. I wasn't even hungry. 'And we did take that car, so it's this huge mess.'

Doug frowned as he listened. He sat opposite me and took a sip of tea from the flowery pink tea cup. 'Well, unfortunately, some people can be bought, whether they're a police officer or not. That's obviously what happened with this fella. I've called David–'

'What did he say?' Lucas interrupted.

'I've called David,' he continued patiently. 'I told him what you'd already told me, and he's making some calls. I'll ring him back shortly. He's agreed to keep this off the books, by the way. At least until we know who's involved. So, tell me more.'

I wanted to ask about David, but kept my mouth shut. I'd ask Lucas later.

'Okay, well last night,' Lucas said, his mouth full, 'Richards would've known where Coates was the whole time and was making out that he was looking for him.'

'I wonder what he told the woman,' I said, picking up my own tea cup.

'What woman?' Doug asked.

'The woman who came with Constable Richards last night. She wasn't with him this morning.'

'Did you get her name?'

'No.'

Lucas shook his head.

'Unless she was dodgy too.' I took a sip of hot, rich tea.

'We didn't know who to go to this morning,' Lucas said.

'I know, mate.' Doug cradled the small tea cup in his large palm. The way Lucas had done with my espresso cups a lifetime ago. 'Tell me everything that happened from the beginning. Then I'll call David back. He's a good mate, you can trust him.'

We replayed the last twenty-four hours for Doug, beginning with when I saw Graham Coates outside the clinic. I told him everything I could remember about going home and finding him there, waiting for me. What he said, how he attacked me and dragged me towards his car. What he said about cutting my throat and making Lucas watch. I realised as I was talking that Lucas hadn't heard this, at least not from me. The growing horror on his face told me he hadn't known all the details. He held his sandwich halfway to his mouth; he seemed frozen in space. It was as though he wasn't even there but was somewhere else, safe in a bubble where all this shit couldn't break through to him.

'I don't really remember much after that except everyone appeared at my place. I sat on the couch while they all talked to the paramedics and the police. Right, Lucas?'

Lucas shook his head then and began filling in the gaps.

When Doug had all the pieces, he excused himself from the table and retreated to an unseen part of the house to call his friend. Alone in the kitchen, Lucas dragged his chair closer to me. He squeezed my hands between his and lifted them towards his face, pausing with them only millimetres away from his split lip.

'I wish I could kiss you,' he murmured.

'You hadn't heard the details, had you?'

He shook his head.

'Are you okay? I've been so worried about you.' I was whispering, aware that Doug may be able to hear. I withdrew my hands, and then, noticing the flash of hurt, I touched my fingertips to his forehead. 'Are you all right?' I asked again.

'I'll be all right.'

'We'll look after each other.' I nodded, to reassure myself as well.

'Does your head still hurt?'

'Yes. But it's not as bad now we've stopped driving.' I paused. 'Doug seems really nice.'

He exhaled. 'I hope he can fix this.' He pushed out of his chair and walked to the window, bracing his hands across the sink. He was leaning forward and stretching out his leg. 'You asked about the view? Come look,' he said over his shoulder.

My own legs leaden, I walked to the window. A film of dust or salt covered the glass, and through it ... something inside of me crumbled. Doug's house was perched on top of a hill, the ocean spread out before him. Over the tops of the trees, an expanse of blue as far as I could see. It was like being inside a box in the sky.

My breath tunnelled out of me, and the heaviness that

remained in my head evaporated. Beside Lucas, I gripped the edge of the sink and jammed my nails against the stainless steel.

'Beautiful, isn't it? If things weren't so ... I'd take you down there to the beach. There's a track. Or we could drive into town and take the main entrance to the beach. It's really nice. Do you know how to surf?'

Sweat had broken out on my lower back. I was concentrating on my breathing but it wasn't working. *In, out, in, out* ... Lucas was frowning at me. 'No, I don't know how to surf.' I turned away and grabbed a sandwich, biting into ham, and cucumber and lettuce. It was so much tastier than the half-stale bread at the service station, but I had to force myself to swallow the mouthful. The nausea had returned, cinching my throat tight. Unsteady, my head kicked around, once, twice. Today was too big, that's what it was. I could have died today. And now every time I looked through the window or stepped outside, the ocean was there to taunt me. How could I possibly explain *that* to Lucas?

'Hey.' There he was in front of me. 'You feel sick again?' He peered into my face.

I tried to smile to reassure him, but my lips wouldn't obey. Voices were clanging through my memory, and one of them was his, accusing me of flinching from his touch. I never wanted it more, and not just for comfort, but so I wouldn't have to keep talking. So I lowered the sandwich and hugged him, burying my face into the warmth of his neck. The collar of his jacket was torn, the edges of it frayed and tickling the end of my nose. In my makeshift cave of tangled hair and fabric, I could smell the old sweat and the old fear on him.

'We're safe here,' he said into my hair.

Doug cleared his throat from the doorway. 'Sorry to interrupt, but David wants to talk to you, mate.'

Lucas and I parted. 'Yeah?'

'Some questions I can't answer.'

Doug sat back at the table with a heavy sigh. 'Amanda, please eat something.'

I picked up the sandwich I'd dropped on the table and forced it back into my mouth. 'I'm not very hungry,' I said, trying not to choke on the bread.

Doug pulled out the chair next to him and grazing a sandpapery hand against my elbow, guided me into it. 'I know, darl, but you'll feel sick later if you don't.'

'What's he asking Lucas?'

He tapped his fingertips against the tabletop. 'Oh, some details about the car accident.'

The stodgy lump of bread moved sluggishly down my throat. 'What did you tell him?'

'Everything you told me.' Doug kept drumming his fingers. 'What's important is the information about Richards. If they can get him to cooperate, he can lead them to Coates.'

'Do you think so?'

'I do.'

'How long do you think it will take to find him?'

He smiled at me. 'I wish I knew.' He cleared his throat and swiped a hand across his eyes; I'd seen Lucas do that too. 'But I know one thing. Lucas won't take you back home unless it's safe.'

'You're worried?' I picked out a slice of cucumber and sucked on it. At least it was cold and wouldn't get stuck in my throat.

Doug took a deep breath. 'Someone like Coates is unpredictable, that's what worries me.' He held up his hands. 'If he has these ideas about revenge, and he's got the money to pay off someone like Richards, well ...'

Finally I put down the sandwich. 'Are we safe here?'

'Oh yes. I wouldn't want to see you at your place though, or Luke's.' He frowned at me. 'You shouldn't have stayed at home after he assaulted you.'

'I know. But Lucas and Marianne were there, and Constable Richards was aware of it. Although, you know, we assumed we could trust him.' I shook my head. 'Did they patrol the neighbourhood like he said? Or was it all a lie?'

'A report was made, Amanda. He followed normal procedure, for the most part.'

Lucas limped back into the kitchen. 'David's calling as soon as he gets anything.'

'He didn't want to talk to me?' I asked.

Lucas shrugged, but didn't say anything.

Doug clapped his hands together. 'Right then. Let's have a look at you both.' He turned to me. 'Amanda, can I take a look at that bump on your head?'

I glanced at Lucas. He was leaning against the wall, arms crossed.

'Okay.'

Doug curled a hand under my chin. 'How do you feel? Headache?'

'Yes, but it isn't too bad. Not like last night.'

He parted my hair, which had already become sweaty and stringy from the morning we'd had. As soon as he found the bump, I flinched. It was still tender, hot and fragile.

'Not as big as last night,' I heard Lucas say.

'Good.' He nudged Lucas. 'Take off your shirt.'

I moved away, squatting next to Bessie who was curled up under the table. Lucas took off his shirt and slung it over the back of a chair.

'Take a deep breath.'

A sharp intake of air, followed by a small cough. 'Shit, that hurts.'

'Do it again.'

'It hurts.' Another breath, cut short. I looked over. Doug was holding Lucas around the shoulders while he pressed a hand into his ribs.

'But it doesn't hurt to breathe normally?'

'No.'

'I don't think anything's fractured. Sit down so I can get this glass out.' Doug moved behind Lucas with a pair of tweezers. Curiosity got the better of me and I moved over to have a look. The scratches on his back were red and swollen, and my stomach turned as Doug gripped the tweezers and slid a piece of glass from one of them. A bubble of blood ballooned and quick as a flash, Doug whipped a folded handkerchief from his pocket and dabbed the cut with it.

'We'll have to get some antiseptic on them, but not 'til you've had a shower.'

*

While Lucas showered, Doug and I sat on the couch with Bessie. Doug had found some old clothes in a cupboard that had once belonged to Lucas and Ben, and neatly folded, they sat on the coffee table for me to change into.

I waited, hands on knees, for Lucas to finish. I could hear

the water running in the bathroom, and it took every part of me not to imagine Lucas standing naked underneath it. Beside me, Doug patted Bessie's head while humming a tune I didn't recognise.

'Do you mind me asking *you* something?' he said.

'Sure.'

'Where are your folks? You've been talking about your friends, but haven't mentioned family.'

'They live in Sorrento. I don't see them much.'

He raised his eyebrows, waiting for me to continue.

'I'm an only child, and not very close to my mum and dad.'

'Ah, that's a shame. You haven't told them what's happening then?'

I shook my head. I could imagine the phone call – Mum shrieking about how stupid I was to get involved with someone like this, that it was like Marco all over again. She didn't even know the details about Marco yet managed to use him as an example. And all the while, the man she had admired outside Alberto's was the very man who had caused all of this. A man similar to Marco, at least in Marianne's opinion.

'My mum and I don't get along, and I can't really talk to my dad.'

Doug clicked his tongue against his teeth. 'I'm sorry to hear that, love.'

'Can I ask you something? Who's the lady in all the pictures?' I pointed to the mantelpiece and the dust-free shrine of framed photos.

Doug smiled, and I could see pure love. 'That's my wife, Ann. Oh, what a woman she was. It's been years since she died, but I like to think she moved up here with me. She loved it here.'

'I don't think Lucas has mentioned her.'

'Hmmm, well, they got along like a house on fire, those two. Ben as well. We couldn't have any of our own kids, and the boys were alone a lot. Their mother Patsy liked to travel, and would take off ...' His eyes flashed with anger. 'But we loved looking after them, so in the end it all worked out.'

'What was Lucas like when he was younger?'

'Oh, let's see,' Doug sighed. 'He was a serious boy. He was more like Patsy than Ben was, I suppose, interested in art and all that. Ben was more into sport. But Lucas played footy and cricket at school, and he loved the water. He loved coming here to go surfing.'

'Yeah, I saw the photo over there.'

'I can imagine him living on the beach one day, having his own coffee shop or whatever it is he wants to do. He's good with people, and people have always liked him. I thought he might end up out this way, but we'll see.'

'I've only known him a week. I don't know much about him, really.'

Doug frowned at me. 'Look, he's a good boy. He's never attracted trouble. Don't think for a minute he's someone you should avoid. You can trust him.'

I stared at him. How did he know what I was thinking? Could he sense I had issues with trust, or that I doubted him? Maybe it was the policeman in him – analysing my body language and facial expressions.

'I don't know what to think anymore,' I finally said.

'This Graham Coates is the problem, not Luke. And if you want to know the truth, I've never seen Luke look at someone like he does you.'

'Really?' Heat climbed my neck, but I didn't care.

'Absolutely. He had a girlfriend in high school, and they were together for years, but it's different with you. I know my boy. I know how his mind works.'

I couldn't help but smile.

'I'm relieved he brought you up here to me,' Doug continued. 'Not that I can guarantee anything, especially now I've retired. But I still want to look after him, even now that he's grown up. After the accident, I wanted to help. It killed me seeing him like that.'

'You saw him?'

'Not at first. Cam was with him, and brought him up here once he could travel. Luke told me about Coates coming into his hospital room and screaming at him, threatening to hurt him.' Doug shook his head, his lips pursed. 'I know what it's like to lose a wife, and how grief can tear you apart, but there's something that's broken inside that man. There has to be.'

Broken. That was the word. Grief could break some people, and maybe they could never be repaired. Is that what had happened to Coates? Would he keep going until he killed us?

Lucas wandered into the room, dressed in old navy blue tracksuit pants. He clutched a T-shirt in a fist, and his wet hair was dripping down his bare chest as he bent over to pat Bessie. 'Did you want to put anything on my back?' he asked Doug.

Doug boosted himself to his feet. 'Amanda, help yourself, love. There are towels in the cabinet in the bathroom.'

Lucas met my eyes as I stood, and before I looked away

I tried to recognise what Doug had talked about. *'I've never seen him look at anyone the way he does you.'* I still couldn't quite believe it, even though I knew early on that he had feelings for me. Why was it so difficult for me to trust him?

I picked up the clothes from the coffee table, and headed through the kitchen and into the bathroom. It was the first time I'd been alone all day, except for the brief moment in the bathroom at the petrol station. I leaned against the door and breathed in the steamy air. Lucas had just been in here, washing the sweat and the blood from his skin. And finally, I was able to do the same – wash away the memory with the hope that Doug and his calm ways could make everything better.

The bathroom was small and cluttered, with the sink and attached cabinet taking up the majority of the room. I wiped the steam from the mirror and peered into it. I looked haggard. The bruise was a dark patch on my cheek, my eyes sunken and shadowed, my skin pasty white, and my lips dry and pressed together.

I found a rolled-up towel in the cupboard underneath, stripped off my clothes, and turned on the water. I stepped onto the bathmat, onto a wet imprint of Lucas's feet. I lined up my heels with his, where he had stood only minutes earlier, naked and dripping. *Oh God.*

I couldn't get Doug's words out of my head. All said with such conviction about Lucas being trustworthy, and how things were different with me. But I couldn't stop thinking about Coates either. Grieving and broken. Doug had made him sound almost human, but what I had seen in his eyes – in the house this morning and outside my apartment, the anger, the hatred – it wasn't what I'd call human. Broken seemed like an understatement.

I climbed into the shower and closed the curtain. The shampoo bottle was wet with suds still foaming from the top. I massaged some into my scalp, avoiding the tender lump as much as possible. I reached for the soap – a silver-grey scratchy bar – rubbed it quickly over my body, and stood under the water. I pressed my palms against the still-warm tiles, trying not to think about Graham Coates, or Doug tending to Lucas's injuries, or Lucas himself. But ... he had stood here before me, with the same shampoo running down his back.

'I've never seen him look at anyone the way he does you.'

I closed my eyes.

Stop.

Chapter 12

I dressed in clothes that had once belonged to Lucas. Grey trackies and a black Nike jumper. They were far too big, and I rolled the pants up at the ankles before I left the bathroom.

Doug stood near a boiling kettle and smiled. 'Feel better?'

'Yes, thanks.'

'Did you leave your clothes in there? I'll wash them and have them dry for you by the morning. I can do your delicates too, if you like. Just leave them in there.'

I leaned over to peck him on the cheek. 'I have, thanks.'

Somehow it wasn't awkward to imagine Doug rinsing through my underwear, and in this moment, I was grateful that Lucas had brought us up here into this warm little house by the ocean.

*

We sat down for dinner on the couch, balancing plates of bangers and mash on our laps while our clothes dried on the horse in front of the fire. Doug's friend David hadn't called, and his number had gone straight to voicemail when Doug had tried. He assured us that was a good sign, he was out there searching, and we would hear from him as soon as anything changed. I decided to believe him, and at least for tonight, relax enough to catch up on some of the sleep I'd been missing.

'I feel bad about the spare room,' Doug was saying. 'There's so much junk in there, but the mattress should be right.'

'We'll work it out, don't worry,' Lucas answered.

I sopped up some gravy with a piece of sausage, keeping one eye on the TV. It was down low, the news mumbling about something irrelevant that happened in parliament. Maybe if I watched long enough they'd put up a sketch or photo of Graham Coates – beam him into everyone's homes with a Crimestoppers number to help the police hunt him down. But I didn't want him beamed into Doug's home. I wanted to curl up in front of the fireplace and wait for the phone to ring with good news.

*

I phoned Marianne before bed, tiptoeing out onto the front veranda. It was freezing, and I had no socks. I curled up cross-legged on a chair, shielding my bare feet.

'It's me.'

'Thank God. Tell me everything.'

'There's nothing to tell, really. Doug's called some old contacts and told them about Jason Richards and everything else. We're waiting to hear back.'

Marianne huffed into the phone. 'Are you all right?'

'Yeah. Doug's a sweet man.'

'How's Lucas?'

'He's okay, I think. Doug's like this first aid pro, and had to pull some glass out and stuff.'

'Shit.' She sighed. 'I wish I could do something. I'm gonna go mental waiting.'

I smiled. '*You* are?'

'So what is it like there? It's a small town, right?'

'The town is small, but we're not in town. Doug's house is out of town, right on the water.'

'The water? As in the ocean?'

A shiver tingled up my spine. 'That's right.'

Another huff into the phone. 'How are you going to go with that?'

'Well, I don't have much choice. If they can catch them ... hopefully this will be over really soon and I can come home.'

'So, his house is ... what, isolated?'

'Yeah.'

'That's not good, honey.'

'What other choice do we have?'

'Yeah. Okay. It's just that you're in the middle of nowhere with a man you don't know, and let's face it, you don't know Lucas either, as it turns out.'

My stomach tilted. The cold air was burning my fragile throat and I swallowed hard. 'What are you doing? Don't say that shit to me.'

'I'm sorry. But it's true–'

'Don't!' I snapped. My voice had risen and my free hand clenched into a fist in my lap. 'Seriously. I'm the one who's stuck here. How is it helping if you say shit like that?'

'You're right, I'm not helping. Shit, I'm sorry. Maybe I can come up there and be with you.'

'You know you can't do that. He could be watching you now, and follow you up here.'

'This is insane, this is like ...' she trailed off, but she didn't really need to find an analogy.

'I know.'

Doug's work shed was a looming shadow. It was so still out the front of the house. Creepy still. Lucas had mentioned that it got really windy here, but tonight there wasn't a breath of it. The trees were barely visible at the edges of the property, their skeletons frozen against the sky. I shivered in the quiet.

'Call me tomorrow. As soon as you hear anything.'

'I will. Same here, if anything happens back there. Is Cam okay?'

'Yeah, we're looking out for each other. Try to get some sleep.'

'Okay. Love you.'

'Love you, too.'

Lucas and Doug had made up the couch with a blanket and pillow, and another bed had been assembled on the carpet beside it. Bessie was on her side in front of the fireplace, panting. I passed Lucas his phone and sank down in front of the roaring fire, stretching my hands and feet out to warm them.

'Any news?' he asked.

'Nope.'

Doug shuffled into the room, carrying a tray. 'Hot chocolate for everyone.'

I took a mug and wrapped my hands around it.

'Real chocolate. Seventy percent. Cut up fine, with hot milk poured over it.' Doug nodded, and seemed to be waiting for me to taste it.

I took a sip; its silky warmth soothed my throat. 'It's beautiful.'

'Good then, that's good.' He locked the front door, sliding the dead bolt, and turned off the lights, leaving only the warm orange glow of the fire. 'Anything you need, just sing out, you two. I'll try David again first thing in the morning.' He took a mug for himself and patted his leg. 'Bess.'

The dog leapt to her feet and trotted after Doug. They disappeared from the room, down the hallway off the kitchen. I heard a door close.

Lucas grunted as he struggled to lower himself onto the mattress set up on the floor. I helped him, hooking him under the arms. Once under the blanket, he reached for his mug of hot chocolate.

'You don't mind if I take the mattress? I need to keep my leg stretched out.'

'No, whatever you want. You're the one who's hurt.'

'So are you.' He pulled his lower lip into his mouth, sucking on it.

'No, I'm all right.' I held a hand against a temple. I'd taken some Nurofen earlier, so it wasn't too bad. 'Are you going to be able to sleep?'

'Don't worry.'

I finished my chocolate and crawled onto the couch. It was a bit awkward now that Doug had gone to bed. He'd kept us busy – feeding us and cleaning us up. If he could do anything, it was to nurture those in his company. I was warmed through, inside and out. I didn't know him

– Marianne was right – but I trusted him, and I already understood the bond between him and Lucas. I rested my head on the cool pillowcase. I could hear Lucas moving around, and his sigh as the movements stopped.

'Amanda?'

I rolled onto my side to face him. He had propped himself on an elbow.

'Are you okay?' he asked. He was close enough that I could smell shampoo. But with his back to the fire, his face was cast in shadow. 'You feel okay being here?'

I considered his question. It was irrelevant, I thought, because what could he do if I said no? 'We don't have much choice, do we?' I whispered back.

'Everything will get sorted out, I promise.'

'Don't promise,' I hissed, sounding angry when I wasn't. I wanted him to know I trusted him, trusted Doug, and that I felt as comfortable as I possibly could in this situation. But how could I when instinct screamed at me to shut up and protect myself? My independence had been stolen from me last night, and not one day later, here I was, three hours from home inside a strange man's house at the beach. I probably *should* have been angry, but everything Lucas had done, and Doug for that matter, was to protect me, to save my life.

Lucas wasn't saying anything and it didn't help that I couldn't see his expression.

'Sorry,' I said, trying to keep my voice soft. 'I'm not mad.' I swallowed, trying to form the words first in my exhausted mind before I said something to make things worse. 'I'm not used to relying on other people, you know, new people that I haven't known for a long time. But I know you're trying to help me.'

He braced himself against the edge of the couch, resting his chin on his arm. 'It's me too, Amanda.'

'What do you mean?'

'I'm trying to help *me* too.' He sighed. 'I'm trying to do what's best for both of us.'

I sat up. 'I know that.'

'Then come here. I'd come up there, but it's not that easy for me to move right now.'

'I don't–'

'Don't mistake me for an enemy,' he interrupted.

'Don't try and read my mind,' I shot back, my voice echoing over the crackle of flames.

He laughed as he moved away. 'Shit. Sorry.'

I smiled in the dark, and crawled down from the couch. I crossed my legs on the blanket beside him. 'This isn't the ideal way to start a relationship is it?'

He laughed again. 'Nope.' He was leaning back on his hands, his legs stretched out flat in front of him.

'So, what's going to happen with your leg now?'

'I don't know, I guess I'll have to go back into rehab, maybe have more surgery.' His voice quavered a little. Obviously the surgery he'd had wasn't a fond memory.

'Is it hurting right now?'

'Yeah.'

'Can I see it?'

He pulled the blanket aside, and carefully, I helped him roll up his tracksuit pants from the ankle. In the dim light, his knee was swollen. Leaning close, I found the scar, running from the top of his shin and over his knee cap, where it disappeared under the fabric. I trailed my index finger along it, through the pale hair on his leg, stopping when I reached his thigh.

'It doesn't look so bad.'

'It's a bit different on the inside.'

'Can I do anything? Do you want a pillow under it?'

'No, I just want to leave it.'

I glanced back at him. 'I hope you can get some sleep.' I covered his leg again and sat back. I didn't know what time it was, but it felt late. I couldn't remember ever being so tired.

Lucas slid his fingers between mine, and I let him. *I wish I could kiss you*, he'd said to me in the kitchen, hours ago, and I'd pulled away. I squeezed his hand, and he squeezed back. I rose to my knees, used my other hand to cradle his face, and I kissed him.

'Goodnight, Lucas.'

'Goodnight, Amanda.'

Chapter 13

I woke to the smell of smoke and the creak of floorboards. I jerked upright, panting, fear skittering through me. Voices. Lucas and Doug were talking quietly in the kitchen. I was safe. Bessie had replaced Lucas on the mattress, and the fire was low, smoke creeping thin fingers around a massive log. I pushed off the blanket; Lucas's baggy old tracksuit pants were hot. Bessie eyed me calmly as I struggled to step over her, my legs wobbly after lying down so long. I squatted beside her, stroking her head and taking a moment to try and overhear what Lucas and Doug were talking about. I couldn't.

They sat at the kitchen table. Lucas had his leg propped up on a chair and was crunching on an apple. Doug, beside him, was rolling an empty water glass between his palms.

'You're up.' Lucas nudged the extra chair away from under his leg, and I sat.

'What time is it?' Through the window, the sky looked grey and heavy.

'It's nearly eight,' Doug answered, flicking the kettle on.

'And we've got some news. I rang David.'

My stomach flipped. 'They found him.'

Lucas shook his head. 'Jason. They're talking to him, and he's cooperating.'

I spun to Doug. 'What does that mean?'

He was spooning tea leaves into the pot. 'He's admitted he was paid by Graham Coates to get information on you two. The man has huge debts. Gambling. Mortgage. Child maintenance.'

'Has he told them the rest of it? The house and everything?'

Lucas nodded, pushing his hair off his face. 'Coates wasn't there. But they're still talking to Jason.'

'David's organised for an officer to come over here,' Doug said.

'Is that safe?' My stomach twisted at the memory of Constable Richards in uniform, diving on top of Lucas in the back of the police car.

'No one knows where Coates is,' Doug answered. 'We need to keep you two as safe as possible.'

Lucas wrapped an arm around my shoulders and I leaned back against him, letting out a long, slow breath. It was nearly over. I could feel it.

*

We'd finished our breakfast and washed up the dishes and the police officer still hadn't arrived. I agreed to help Doug make some choc chip biscuits to pass the time, but when I admitted I wasn't familiar with baking, he'd shaken his head.

'Don't you work at the restaurant?'

'No. Sometimes I help prepare the meals but I don't bake anything.'

'Marianne told me you make a really good carbonara, though,' Lucas piped up from the table.

'Is that right?' Doug asked. 'So, you cook mains rather than sweets.'

'Well, no, I don't cook much at all, actually.'

Doug chuckled. 'Then aren't you in for a treat? This is a cracker recipe, if I do say so myself.'

He tied an apron around his bulging belly. 'Now, this is Ann's recipe. To be honest, I had to fix it up a bit. She was always a bit heavy-handed with the sugar, and then I realised the chocolate adds its own sweetness, so I adjusted it a little bit.'

I glanced over my shoulder at Lucas, who raised his eyebrows and grinned.

'Can you please cream the butter and sugar together? Grab that wooden spoon there, and use some elbow grease.'

I did what I was told, cradling the bowl in the crook of my arm, while Doug continued to measure out the ingredients.

'I like lots of choc chips in them, but not too many. Some of those fancy ones you get in the supermarkets have too many. You're biting into chocolate, not a biscuit.'

I nodded in reply, as if what he was saying made sense to me. I couldn't remember the last time I'd eaten a choc chip biscuit from the supermarket, and what the chocolate-to-biscuit ratio had been when I'd done so. Most of my sweet treats I sampled at Alberto's. Giovanni's biscotti with almonds were amazing.

Doug was studying my stirring skills, frowning into the bowl. 'Good, now we'll add the egg and the vanilla.'

'Do you want to stir?'

'No, keep going.'

I supported the bowl while he added the flour and choc chips, and when the dough had come together, I helped Doug shape spoonfuls and place them on the trays.

'The trick,' Doug said, 'is to make sure you don't leave them in too long. It's important to swap the trays halfway through and to get them out *just* as they start turning golden. Otherwise they're ruined.' He crouched in front of the oven and slid the trays inside. 'Seven minutes, then we swap.'

Before the first batch had come out of the oven, the phone rang. Doug shuffled through the kitchen door to answer it. Lucas, impatient, followed him and lingered in the hallway. I finished the biscuits, lifting them onto the cooling racks as Doug had instructed. As soon as they were cool enough to touch, I took a bite of one.

'Was that David?' I asked as they returned, my mouth full.

Doug shook his head. 'The station in Hanley. Apparently there's been a car accident on the highway so they can't send anyone over until later this arvo. Maybe not until the morning.'

'The morning? It's only noon.'

'Small town,' Lucas snapped, his eyes narrowed. 'Fucking ridiculous. What are there, two cops in all of Hanley?'

Doug glanced across at him. 'Calm down, mate. Everyone's keeping an eye out for Coates, which is a good thing. Richards is talking. Everything is moving forward. You'll both stay here tonight and take it easy, it'll be fine.'

Lucas sat with a sigh, features softening. 'Yeah, okay.'

Doug nodded at me, and the remaining piece of biscuit

I was holding. 'Well?'

'You were right. These are unbelievable.'

He beamed. 'Told you.'

*

Once the dryer had rattled to a stop, I changed back into my own clothes. When I stepped out of the bathroom, the kitchen was empty, the lounge room too. Even Bessie was missing from the mattress. I spotted Lucas's phone on the couch and went to pick it up, at the same time the front door swung open. Lucas rubbed his red hands briskly together.

'Doug and I are going to fix up the bungalow for tonight. Does that sound okay?'

'What bungalow?'

'Doug has a bungalow down the back there,' he pointed through the kitchen, and the long, steep backyard full of trees, and beyond that, the ocean. 'He thought it'd be more comfortable, rather than sleeping here on the floor.'

'So, you don't think we'll be going home today?'

He shrugged. 'Probably not. Even if they find him today, it's still a few hours in the car.' When I didn't say anything, Lucas continued. 'Doug thought it might be nice to give us our own space or whatever. That's where I sleep whenever I come here. There's a proper bed and everything.'

I shuffled my feet. As much as I liked Doug, I was itching to get home. As each hour passed, it was getting harder to stay positive. The snap of impatience I'd seen with Lucas in the kitchen earlier hadn't helped either. I didn't want to prolong this whole thing by shifting into a bungalow with Lucas. Why couldn't the police find Graham Coates? I just wanted to go home.

'What's wrong?' Lucas asked.

'I don't know, is it safe? I like it here in the house with Doug. You know, moving into a bungalow doesn't feel like a good idea. And I thought we'd be going home by now.'

'Come with me.' He limped into the kitchen, beckoning me to the window. Immediately, my eyes settled on the blanket of dark water. 'See that roof there?' He pointed; a strip of corrugated iron roof and brick chimney was visible through scrubby branches. A worn path through the grass led down the side of the shack and to a couple of steps bordered by what looked like a wooden veranda. 'It's not far from the house.'

He was right. The bungalow and wood shed were the closest two buildings to the house. 'So, just for tonight, right?'

'I hope so. I don't know. Hopefully a cop actually comes from town and has some news.' He squeezed me around the shoulders. 'You want to help? Doug said no one's stayed there for a few months.'

I carried a pile of sheets, pillows and a doona to the bungalow. The grass was getting long on either side of the path, and I lifted my boots trying not to slip. The day was colder than yesterday, the wind churning through the trees around us. At least with the wind though, the sound of the ocean wasn't as audible.

I neared the wood shed with its walls of firewood stacked neatly up to the corrugated-iron roof. Doug and Lucas carried wood towards the bungalow, their shoes clunking along the veranda. I passed the slender shape of an axe, its blade wedged into a giant lump of wood that rested on the ground. I shuddered, keeping my eyes ahead.

As I approached the bungalow, I heard a sliding door open and shut. I took the steps, struggling to see my feet over the pile of linen. I wobbled up onto the veranda, and Doug, seeing me through the glass, opened the sliding door. The bungalow was one large room with a tiny kitchenette off it. One queen-sized bed, mattress bare, sat to my right. I dumped the blankets on it and looked around.

Doug had disappeared, his footsteps echoing along the veranda. Lucas was squatting awkwardly in front of the fireplace, arranging kindling and logs. Beside him on the hearth, a pile of wood had been neatly stacked. The place had a musty smell, but it was nicer than I'd expected. Two cracked-leather recliners by the fire, a table and two chairs; and since it didn't sit high upon the hill, the water wasn't visible from the windows. I opened a nearby door and found a toilet and hand basin in a tiny, tiled, and freezing cold room.

'When was the last time you were here?' I asked Lucas.

'Months ago,' he answered over his shoulder. 'I was here for Christmas. Cam drove me here to stay for a while.'

'After the accident?'

'Yeah.'

He didn't say anything else, and I didn't push. I made up the bed, smoothing the sheets over the mattress. Then I threw on the doona. I shook the two pillows into their cases and tossed them on top. Above the bed, on the wall, hung a landscape painting in a plain gold frame. The beach, rocks, trees, and Doug's house on the hill. The style of painting was familiar.

'Did your mum paint this?'

Lucas glanced over his shoulder. 'Yeah.'

I thought of the Amalfi painting and how I'd left it perched against my bedroom mirror at home, unsure of where I wanted to keep it, concerned that every time I looked at it I'd think of Marco. How irrelevant all that seemed now. How irrelevant Marco seemed in comparison to Graham Coates. Marco was in my past – he had no hold over me anymore. But Graham Coates was a current threat. It struck me then how stupid I'd been, wasting so much time not getting over Marco, dwelling on him. The whole time my days had been numbered. My life had been leading towards the day Lucas walked into Alberto's and unintentionally brought Coates along with him.

Doug returned with food. I helped him unpack the apples, bananas, grapes, milk, bread, margarine, a jar of Vegemite, instant coffee and a Tupperware container packed with the choc chip biscuits. He rummaged through the cupboards, explaining where everything was that we may need. He plugged in the kettle and toaster, and turned the tap on to let it run for a while.

The three of us ate on the veranda, the chilly air nipping at my hands and cheeks. I sipped the bad coffee from a mug that had been wiped of dust, and scanned the row of trees in front of me. The sky shone through a couple of gaps, but I couldn't see the water. I didn't understand how that worked, but figured if I walked closer to Doug's back fence it would be there in all its furious glory.

Nervousness was niggling at me. The cop could have arrived, could be hammering at the front door up the hill. Or the phone could be jangling off the hook at Doug's house, with no one to answer it. I still had so many questions, but Lucas seemed calm, sipping from his mug with his feet propped up on the railing. So I ate grapes instead, tired of asking so many questions, tired of sitting and waiting. Just tired. Maybe I could sleep until Lucas woke me up to tell me it was all over.

*

Once Lucas and I were alone, and Doug had left us instructions to come up to the house for dinner, I fetched the mobile to call Marianne. A low battery warning, despite Lucas switching it off overnight.

'Look,' I said to Lucas, showing him the screen.

He shook his head and sighed. 'These batteries are shit.'

'Should I try and call now or use Doug's phone later?'

He shrugged. 'I talked to Cam before. Maybe call later when we've heard something else. Switch it off.'

I turned the phone off and tossed it on the coffee table. 'Now what?'

'You could go down to the beach for a walk, it's beautiful down there. I'd come, but the track is pretty steep, and I don't know if–'

'No, I don't want to do that.'

'Okay ...' He frowned at me. 'I guess we could sit and talk.'

He'd already dropped into one of the armchairs before I'd answered. So I sat, following his lead and lifting the foot rest to stretch out my legs. 'What do you want to talk about?'

'Actually, I wanna ask you something.' He cleared his throat. 'What is it with you and the water?'

My stomach flipped, and my hands curled into fists. I squeezed them tightly in my lap, fighting the rise of hot terror that was surging up my throat. 'What do you mean?'

He'd rested his chin in his hand and was studying my expression. 'You don't like the ocean, do you?'

I guess I knew that question would come eventually; I just didn't know how to answer it. Leaning back, I flattened my hands against the arms of the chair. 'No, I don't like the ocean.'

'Why?'

I took a breath, exhaling slowly. My mind screamed at me to tell him. *Trust him!* I had to. But those first steps to the truth were the hardest. 'It started when I was little. I always hated the water, not sure why.' I shrugged. 'And then when I was about ten, I was at the beach and this kid drowned. My fear just kind of took over ...'

'Oh. Why didn't you tell me?' His voice was soft and his expression concerned.

I looked away. 'I don't know. There didn't seem to be much point. The water thing has always been there. You know, I saw that, and ... then Marco taking me to Amalfi and Ravello ...'

He waited patiently for me to continue, but I couldn't get the words out.

'I still dream about it,' I said instead. 'Whenever I see the water, I go back in time ... to those weekends, to him.'

'Now I feel bad for giving you that painting. And bringing you here. God, I'm fucking up your life, aren't I?'

I gave him a half-smile. 'Nah, it was already pretty fucked up. And this isn't your fault.'

Some tension dropped from his face, but he still looked wary. 'So what happened with Marco?'

I picked at my fingernails, trying to form the words. I didn't want to hold back now, not after all that had happened. It was time to tell him, to let him in. 'We went to the coast for weekends sometimes. And I was fine at first. I mean, I was always a bit weird whenever I got close to the actual water. And he wanted to take me out on a boat, but I wouldn't go. He'd get so annoyed. But it was so much fun, driving up there. You know about that?' Lucas shook his head. 'The roads are steep and winding, and there's only room for one car most of the time. But the cars still squeeze past each other, folding their mirrors in as they go. And I swear, it was fun, like the car could tip off the edge if we weren't careful. He'd drive pretty fast, and it was exciting.'

Lucas was quiet. I leaned back against the seat and closed my eyes.

'But then, once everything was over with him, the memory of going there became so dark, and the water thing just got out of control ...' I trailed off. It was too hard to explain. How could I tell him that when I first returned home from Italy that I couldn't even look at a body of water without freaking out? That I couldn't take baths without descending into a panic attack? Now that I could handle it – most of the time – the whole thing felt ridiculous. My insistence of not dealing with what Marco actually did mutated into my childhood fear.

'What did he do to you?'

My hands had begun to sweat, and I wiped them over my jeans and tried to slow my breathing. I wanted to prove to myself and to Lucas that I could trust him. I had to tell him. I had to keep talking, no matter what. 'When he hired me at his bar, I was a novelty, being from Australia and all. Everyone I met there warned me not to get too close to him, but I didn't listen. He started to take me on holidays, and buy me all these gifts. We were at Amalfi on the pier, and he proposed. But the more I got to know him ... I didn't know how to get myself out of it.'

'Wait, so you said yes?'

'I said yes. I was an idiot. I was completely prepared to give everything up and stay there to be with him. Give up my friends – everything. But it wasn't real, it was manipulation. He'd worked his way into my head and somehow gained control over me.' I shook my head, my face blazing with embarrassment. 'He was loaded, he had all this hidden money, and the deeper I got, the more he'd tell me how much he loved me. And I ... I trusted him.'

'So, how did you get out of it?'

'I tried to talk to him about it. Said I couldn't marry him, that I was too young. But he brushed me off. We were at Amalfi for the weekend and he said we should enjoy ourselves and talk about it when we got back. He wanted to take me out on a boat to see these caves, but I said no. He lost it.'

'And?' His voice was soft.

I sucked in a sharp breath. 'He threw me in the water.'

'Fuck,' Lucas breathed.

My heart pounded against my chest, and I sucked in air like I had that day – panicked. 'I knew it wasn't an accident, because I'd seen the anger on his face. There were all these people crowding around on the pier watching, and he jumped in after me. He grabbed my arms and I thought he was trying to pull me out. The water was so rough and cold ... but he held me there. He wouldn't let me get out.'

Lucas gaped. 'What?'

'I could hear people, but they were ... distant, like I wasn't really there. And I had this moment of clarity ... I knew then I could never trust another person with my life. That I never would again. It was all up to me. I had to get myself out of this, but I was at his mercy and he knew it. He was so angry; I was certain I was about to die.'

'Amanda–'

'I'm sorry.' I shook my head. My face was dripping with sweat, and I rubbed my hands over it. 'He did get me out. I guess if there'd been no one around ... well, I don't know.'

'What happened? What did you do?'

'I pretended it was an accident, waited until we got back to the city, and then I left.'

'You came home?'

'I had to borrow money from a friend. I was scared about what he might do, so I didn't tell him. I caught the first flight out of there. I tried to pretend that everything was okay, you know. I never heard from him again.' I dragged in as much oxygen as I could. I felt cold all over. Funny how easily it could all come spilling out of my mouth once I started to speak. And now it was out, and Lucas knew, and I couldn't take it back.

'I'm so sorry you had to go through that.'

'I didn't want to tell you. I don't like talking about it.' I tried to smile, but my dry lips cracked. I finally looked across at him.

'No ... things make a bit more sense now.' He tilted his head, watching me, gaze gentle. 'I wish I hadn't been on your back about Marco. I didn't know about any of it, the water or anything, until now. Marianne never said a thing.'

'I wish I wasn't such a mess.'

'You're not though,' he said, shaking his head. 'You're not

a mess.'

'That was two years ago, and I'm still having nightmares about him. I'm still freaking out when I see water. That's messy shit right there.'

'Fuck, you're allowed. And now, with all this ...' he trailed off. He didn't need to finish. Reaching over, we grasped hands across the coffee table.

Chapter 14

With no word from anyone, I headed up to the house to call Marianne. I leaned against the wall in the hallway as the phone rang and rang, unanswered.

Doug's bedroom was opposite where I stood. Ann's photo hung in an elaborate frame on the wall above his bed, which had been made with military precision. The whole room was as neat as a pin.

I dialled her number again and she finally answered, breathless.

'Hello?'

'It's me.'

'I'm at work. Let me go out the back.'

I waited until I heard the heavy clunk of the metal door sliding open, then the whisk of alley breeze. 'Okay.'

'You're at work early.'

'I'm prepping. I need to keep busy. I haven't heard from you.'

'That's because there's no news. I'm losing it.'

'What do you mean? They're talking to that cop, aren't

they? Cam rang me this morning.'

'Yeah, and he's talking. Someone is supposed to come from the police station in town to see us, but that hasn't happened yet. David said he'd call back when they find Coates, and he hasn't called.'

'So they can't find the fucker.'

'I guess not.'

'Shit. Come home.'

'I want to. I really want to. I mean, Doug's so sweet, and I *do* feel comfortable here. He's keeping us busy, which is good, but nothing's changing and I want things to get back to normal.'

'Have you talked to Lucas?'

'Yeah, and this place is like his home, so he feels really safe here and wants to stay until they find Coates.'

'Just do it, then. I guess.'

'But–'

'Look, I believe you if you say that Doug is nice and all. If it was me though, I'd fucking leave. I couldn't stand it.'

'I can't leave when things are like this, can I? I can't leave Lucas with his hurt leg, and Doug's been so nice–'

'It's your life, and you need to be where you feel safe, honey. If it was me, I wouldn't want to be in an isolated place like that, near the water if that was a problem for me, you know.'

'There you go using that word again.'

'Water?'

'Isolated.'

'Well, you told me that's what it is. You've just met this Doug guy, and you're at the beach, for fuck's sake. All the while some psycho has assaulted you and has threatened to kill you both. How could you possibly be relaxed?'

I clenched my teeth. 'I have to go, I can't talk about this.'

Her voice rose a notch. 'Don't hang up. Keep talking to me.'

'You know, I told Lucas about the water thing. I told him about Marco.'

'You did? Wow.'

'I know.'

'So, you must trust him then. Only a few of us know about–'

'He asked me. He asked me if I was scared of the ocean, and I didn't see the point in denying it when we're stuck in this nightmare. So, I told him about Amalfi, and then he asked about Marco. I just kept talking and it all came pouring out.'

Marianne was quiet a moment. 'That's good, honey,' she said eventually.

'Is it?' I bit my lip, fighting tears.

'Isn't it?'

'I don't know. I'm so confused.'

'About Lucas?'

I nodded, then remembered she couldn't see me. 'Yeah,' I croaked. 'Why couldn't I meet him when things were normal? I feel like I have to cling to him because this arsehole wants his revenge or some shit, but that's not my fault.'

She sighed into the phone. 'You've got people looking for him. When they find him, then I guess things can be normal.'

'What if they don't find him? What if he finds us? What if–'

'They'll find him. It's their job. They'll find him.' Her voice was firm.

'I'm scared,' I whispered. I shouldn't have said it when she was so far away and couldn't do anything. I shouldn't have admitted it, either. I wanted to be brave, to be strong, and prove I could withstand this.

'Me too,' she said.

I swallowed, surprised. Marianne admitting she was scared about anything was a big deal. My stomach turned. 'Do you really think it will be okay?'

'Yes,' she answered.

'You think I can handle this?'

'Fuck yes. You're smart. Trust your instincts, babe. If you need to come home, do it. If you need to stay, then do that. I can help you do anything, you just need to ask.'

'Okay.'

'Call me back as soon as you hear anything.'

'I will.'

I hung up, and peeked through into the kitchen. I couldn't see Doug or Lucas, and I couldn't hear them either. Sniffing, I rested my forehead against the wall and tried to remember everything Marianne had said. Instincts. I needed to trust my instincts.

*

I buttoned my jacket then wrapped Oscar's scarf around my neck, knotting it in front. The afternoon was still so I wanted to do this before the wind picked up. I *needed* to do this. I had to trust my instincts. And they were telling me to stay strong, to prove that I *was* strong. I'd lived in Italy by myself; I hadn't known anyone when I'd arrived. And in Melbourne, too, I'd always taken care of myself, regardless of what my mother believed.

I could do this.

Lucas hugged me. 'I'll wait here on the veranda. Yell if you need me.'

Nodding, I turned away. I didn't *want* to need him. I had to do this by myself.

Setting off through the trees, I found the sandy track and wound my way towards it. Lucas had said it wasn't a long walk, that it should only take a few minutes, but it was steep and should be taken slowly. I wondered if he would even hear me if I had to yell for help, then pushed away the thought.

I walked blindly forward. I couldn't see the water, and it wasn't cold with all the scrubby trees surrounding me. Twigs snatched at my arms, at my boots, but I stormed on with my hands buried deep in my pockets. As the track became steeper, I slowed, bracing my feet when I needed to. I could feel my surroundings change – the drop in temperature, the moisture building. The air felt thick. The smell of salt overpowered me. I struggled to take a breath.

The water appeared suddenly; a sweep of charcoal grey across the landscape. Closing my eyes briefly, I shut out the view. It was too much. I breathed in the air first, acclimatising myself, driving my fists deeper into my jacket. I opened my eyes and walked slowly towards the water, my boots sliding through the soft sand.

It was a narrow strip of beach. Very different to the wide Aussie beaches I remembered from my childhood; this was more like the beaches in Italy. I scanned the length of sand, remembering what Lucas had said about how private it was. He was right. Cliffs jutted out either side, so I couldn't see endless sand and shoreline that stretched on forever.

About halfway to the water, I stopped and squatted in the sand. I scooped up a handful and let it filter between my fingers, watching the grains fall back to my feet. It was kind of beautiful. All this sand, all this pale softness. The sand was gentle, but the ocean – the waves, the salt, the endlessness of it, was something else entirely.

Pushing to my feet, I walked closer, stepping onto damp, compacted sand. My boots left prints as I took each step in slow motion, the air growing thicker and wetter, the salt stinging my nostrils. My chest constricted, shooting pain rolling out like a wave. *Too much.* I leaned forward, bracing my hands on my knees and dragging in a breath as slowly as I could. Why was I doing this? Why did I have to prove this to myself now?

Because it's now or never.

I forced myself to stand up straight and stare out ahead. The horizon was an indistinct blur of grey water and sky. No boats out there dotting the sea, nothing.

I needed to touch the water. Like an enraged beast that haunted my dreams, I needed to make physical contact. To make my peace with it, make a point. Heal myself. Breathing hard, I dipped in a finger. The water was icy, but nothing else. I added one finger at a time until my hand was submerged. I pressed my palm flat against the bottom as the water rushed around my wrist, dampening the sleeve of my jacket, licking at my boots.

I was okay. I was doing it. I thought of Lucas then, waiting for me on the veranda of the bungalow. I thought of Coates – hiding, or whatever he was doing – fucking up my life and stopping me from going home. I thought of Marianne, taking extra shifts at the restaurant so she could distract herself from her fears. And Marco, the person who'd pushed me over the edge long before I knew who Graham Coates was.

And the tears fell, dropping into the water as I bent over with one hand underneath the surface, confronting my fear. My salt mixed in, and symbolically maybe there was some beauty in that.

I sat on the sand for a long time, shaking my hand repeatedly, wiping it against my jeans until it was completely dry. My eyes felt raw from the tears and the air, the breeze swirling grains of sand, building, building. I didn't know what time it was, but I didn't want to go back just yet. The solitude was something I'd been missing, and even though I didn't really *want* it here, I clung to it. I cried; the sound of my sobs collected by the swish of the water. And I didn't care how much sound I made, or what I looked like. That was what I was missing: a place to be alone and cry, to be afraid, to curse the situation, and hate Coates. Hate Richards. Hate Marco. Hate everyone and everything for a few moments; embrace how I was really feeling until my time was up and I had to put on a brave face again.

My limbs were stiff with cold when I found the gap in the trees and started to walk back. The light had dimmed, the wind was screeching, the water's surface was rougher than before. I rubbed at my face as I walked. The icy air had already dried my tears, but my face felt swollen. I didn't want Lucas to know I'd been crying.

He was sitting on the veranda steps in the dusky light, leg

stretched out and frown creasing his forehead. He jumped up as soon as he saw me, meeting me at the edge of the bungalow.

'Are you all right?'

'I'm fine,' I answered, letting him pull me into his arms.

'You're freezing,' he murmured. 'Your face is all red.'

'I'm okay.' I breathed in his warmth.

'We should go up to the house,' he said into my hair. 'David called.'

*

'They can't find him.'

I sat at Doug's kitchen table, my heart pounding. Lucas sat beside me, watching my reaction. He had learnt this while I'd been down on the beach feeling sorry for myself, so maybe he'd had time to process it. Whatever the reason for his calm demeanour, it pissed me off.

'Why not?' My voice was higher than normal. I pushed back out of my chair so I didn't have to look at Lucas. I faced Doug instead, who was cooking toasted sandwiches, spatula in hand. A huge pot of soup simmered on the stove, releasing steam into the already stifling kitchen.

'He may have left town, but he's probably hiding out with a friend. They're doing everything they can, but it might take a couple more days. David said to hold tight.'

I swallowed hard. It was almost dark and I felt exposed by the window – Doug's box in the sky. 'So what do we do now? Did anyone come while I was gone?'

Lucas shook his head. 'They said they'll be here probably first thing in the morning.'

'This is stupid. They're the police! What the hell are they doing?'

Doug blinked, and glanced over at Lucas.

'It'll be okay,' Lucas said.

'Really?' I snapped. 'What evidence have you got?'

Lucas didn't answer and Doug turned back to the sandwiches. I stood in the middle of the kitchen, replaying the conversation with Marianne over in my head. *You've just met this Doug guy, and you're at the beach, for fuck's sake.*

I had to go home. I couldn't just sit here and wait. I'd been trying so hard to pretend I was okay. I'd even gone to the beach, and I thought – stupidly – that I was somehow cured of fear by doing so, that I was strong and could cope with anything. But it felt like this was never going to end.

'You've had a big day,' Lucas said, his eyes narrowing slightly.

I threw up my hands. 'What are you saying?'

'Nothing, just that after some sleep, you might–'

'No.'

'Have a sandwich, love.' Doug held out a plate. Cheese oozed from between the two slices of bread.

'No. No thanks.' I crossed my arms while they both stared at me. Was I the only one upset by this news from David? Didn't Lucas want to go home? 'I'm going back. I'm going to bed.' I glanced at Doug. 'Sorry. I'm going to bed.'

Dew coated the veranda, and my boots slipped as I ran outside. *Why the hell is it taking the police so long to find Coates? It's their job to track down the bad guys. Can't they track his car or credit cards or something?*

At the wood shed, I marched over to the big stump, gripped the handle of the axe and tried to wrestle it free.

It didn't budge. Tugging on it, I growled with the effort. *I need a weapon.* My hands slid uselessly from the handle and I screamed in frustration. The head was jammed into the stump and no amount of rocking or kicking was shaking it loose. I wasn't strong enough.

'Fuck it!'

My decision to conquer my fear by visiting the beach had been rewarded with the news that the police couldn't find Coates. I had done *nothing* to deserve this! Was my life destined to be filled with fear? Was it completely out of my control? I booted the stump as hard as I could, the shockwave jolting through my ankle.

Inside the bungalow, the heat was cloying. I shrugged off my jacket and pelted it into an armchair. Unzipping my boots, I threw them across the room, satisfied when they thundered into the opposite wall. I swore as tears welled up in my eyes for the third time that day. I'd reached my limit, and I couldn't take any more. It ended now.

The sliding door opened and Lucas limped inside. I turned my back and wiped at my eyes, furious with myself for not keeping it together. The sob session on the beach should have helped ease the tension and given me extra strength to get through, but it had only opened the floodgates.

'Amanda.'

'I'm all right.' I kept my voice even, and swiped at my eyes again before I turned to face him. 'Sorry. I'm all right.'

'Doug said if you're worried you can sleep in the house tonight.'

I shook my head, retrieving my boots and placing them right side up by the armchair. I folded my jacket neatly. My stomach knotted, my muscles – all of them – felt tense. The fear was rising and I couldn't breathe. I wiped cold sweat from my face.

'Amanda.'

'I'm going to try and sleep now.' My voice didn't sound right to me. Lucas frowned, but let me go. I crawled on top of the doona, leaving my jeans on, and buried my face into the pillow. I heard Lucas drop into an armchair and sigh. What was he going to do? Sit there and watch over me? Like a bodyguard. A bodyguard with a bad leg. A bodyguard who wouldn't take me home. I rolled onto my belly and clenched my jaw tight. I was acting like a child, but I couldn't help it. The weight of everything squashed the air right out of me. I couldn't breathe. *Panic.*

I staggered to my feet and onto the veranda, where I gripped the railing and let the ocean wind collect my hair. It was freezing, and it was loud, but the air barrelled into me, filling my lungs with much needed oxygen. It was too hot, too suffocating, inside.

'Amanda, it's cold, come inside,' Lucas called through the glass.

'I need a minute,' I replied, my voice disappearing in the whoosh of wind and water. The ocean sounded rough and violent, but for the first time, I didn't care.

'What?'

'I need a fucking minute!' I shouted.

His face fell. The sliding door opened and he stepped through. 'What are you doing?' he asked, frustrated. Steam lingered before his lips with each breath, the pool of light from inside swelling and receding as he hovered in the doorway.

I turned, and something as heavy as iron clamped down

over my chest. My vision swam, and Lucas wavered, no more than a dark blur. He was becoming a sinister shadow, more jailer than bodyguard.

'Trapped,' I whispered.

'What?'

'I can't go in there for a while,' I answered. I blinked to clear my eyes, but when that didn't work, I pressed my knuckles against my eyelids. 'It's hot. I need some space.'

'Okay, but you don't even have your jacket on.'

'God! I want to go home now. I can't stay here anymore. I want to go home.' The words thumped out of me, a force all of their own.

'I know, come here.' He pulled me through the doorway and into the suffocating warmth of the bungalow. His arms were around me, his face close. Heat radiated off him. Too much closeness. 'They'll find him.'

'Yeah, yeah, that's what everyone is saying, and will keep saying, and it makes no difference.'

'It might take a couple more days.'

'I've heard that one before too.' I untangled myself. 'Why can't we just go back,' I pleaded, staring up into his frustrated face. 'We can all be together. Marianne, and Cam, and we won't be so isolated. We'll be in the city and the police will be close by. Safety in numbers and all that. We're so alone here.'

'It's best to stay here. It's not safe for us to be on the road when they don't know where he is, but it's safe here with Doug.'

'You don't know that. How do you know Coates isn't on his way here right now?' I rushed on before he could answer. 'You don't know. You don't know where he is either, so you don't know shit!'

'Jesus,' Lucas groaned. 'We have to trust David, okay? And he said to stay here.' He swiped a hand roughly across his face.

'You know, all this is happening behind my back. I haven't even talked to David, he hasn't told *me* this. I'm just taking your word for it.'

'What are you saying?' Lucas frowned.

'Nothing.' I fell silent, watching him. He stared back, confusion a heavy mask. 'So you really don't want to go home,' I said eventually. 'You want to stay here.'

He nodded. 'I think it's the best thing.'

'What about me? I could take the car and go home without you.'

His frown deepened. 'Do you want to do that? Be on the road alone?'

'It's only a few hours,' I said, then shook my head. 'I just want to go home.'

He didn't say anything.

'You want me to stay here with you and Doug, don't you?'

'Of course–'

'And you've made that decision.'

'What do you mean?' he asked, shifting his weight to his good leg. 'I want you to be safe.'

'It makes more sense to go home and get police help there. Marianne was saying how isolated it is here. We're in the middle of nowhere. You've got me trapped here in this place and I can't leave.' I backed away a few steps.

Lucas froze. 'Trapped? Amanda, what are you talking about?' His tone was careful, his eyes narrowed. He took a few slow steps towards me. 'You can leave if you want. We can call David right now and you can talk to him yourself.'

Ignoring him, I kept retreating until my hips bumped against the glass sliding door. 'Why would you bring me here?' My lower lip trembled. Exasperated, I clamped my teeth onto it.

'You agreed to come here. We both decided, remember? So Doug could help sort this out.'

'But it's not over yet, Lucas!'

'I know, but–'

'You're not listening to me.'

'I am. Don't be ridiculous.'

'Oh,' I cried, sliding along the glass away from him. 'That's right. *I'm* ridiculous. It's not the guy who wants us dead. It's not you who brings us to a fucking shack in the middle of nowhere. No, it's me. *I'm* ridiculous!' My voice had escalated into a hysterical shriek but I couldn't stop it. I flinched as Lucas reached out for me.

'Stop it,' he pleaded, through clenched teeth. 'Stop it. Calm down.' He grabbed my arm, his fingertips digging into my skin.

'I can't,' I panted. 'I feel like I have no say in any of this; that I'm stuck here. I just have to sit here and wait while you and Doug run the show.'

He was shaking his head but I couldn't stop.

'It's like Marco all over again. I try to be strong but everything falls to pieces.' I gasped, hard, choking on the words. I expected anger when I looked into his eyes, but I only saw sadness.

'I'm not Marco. I wouldn't hurt you.' His fingers loosened their grip and his arm fell to his side. Blinking, he backed away, and in that moment I saw myself clearly.

Shit.

Regret crept up on me as I watched him step away, hurt and confused.

Lucas was right. Of course he wouldn't hurt me; he'd done nothing but try to keep me safe. Alive. But this burst of irrational anger distracted me from my biggest fear. I'd had an opportunity to explode and blame someone for everything that was going wrong, and I'd taken it.

'I'm sorry.' I bit my lip as hard as I could, but I couldn't hold back one shuddering groan tearing free from my throat. 'He's going to find us.'

'No.'

'We're going to die.'

'No, we're not.' His voice cracked, and I hung my head. 'We're not going to die.'

I slid slowly to the carpet until I was on my knees. Lucas followed, keeping his right leg stretched out. He smoothed my hair away from my face and made me look at him. 'I'm so sorry about all of this. I'm so sorry.'

Another groan escaped, as the guilt came rushing up my throat. His eyes were wet, the panic clearly etched on his face. And here I was blaming him, comparing him to Marco and Graham Coates. He was broken, like Coates, but in a different way. Coates had messed up Lucas's life too, and he had a permanent injury as a constant reminder.

In the triangle of his legs, I brushed away the tears as they spilled over his cheeks.

'You have to trust me,' he whispered.

Marianne's voice replayed over and over, relentless.

'I do.'

Didn't I? I had to.

Chapter 15

When I woke, Lucas lay beside me on the bed, fully clothed. The wind swirled outside. The fire low and smouldering. Now I wasn't hot, and I didn't feel suffocated. I felt guilty, embarrassed, and stupid. I shivered, rolling onto my side to face him.

'I'm sorry,' I whispered. I didn't know whether he was awake or not, and I didn't expect him to answer if he was. I crawled across the mattress, reaching out until I found his chest. He pulled me to him, wrapping his arms around me. 'Tighter.'

He held me close. His heart beat hard against my ear. My body was pressed against his. Finally, side by side, I didn't feel smaller than him. I felt like his equal – despite my meltdown, despite his tears. I had to stay. We had to support each other. My mouth found his. When he moaned, I pulled back, unsure if I'd hurt his lip.

'Don't stop,' he whispered.

The need built inside of me, and I slid a hand through his soft hair. I wanted him. There were no other thoughts in my head. I moved closer. He was hard against me. He moaned again, arching his hips forward. We managed to tug each other's pants down, and then he was on top of me, inside me, supporting himself with his hands as we moved together.

Our breath and the creaking bed were the only sounds in the dark. There was no time and no point in holding back any longer, and nothing needed to be said. I couldn't see him well, but I didn't need to. In this moment, everything about him was familiar.

The wall I had built years ago to protect myself from being hurt was collapsing, and it didn't fill me with fear. It felt amazing. It was the first thing that made sense for a long, long time.

He rolled over, pulling me with him. We tore off our remaining clothes and I straddled him, the cool air kissing my skin. I let my voice tear free as I threw my head back. I rode him as the wind built outside. As it screamed and rattled the windows, I gripped his hands in mine.

*

A banging sound woke me. I struggled into a sitting position, finding Lucas sitting beside me, his eyes wide. The kitchen light was on, the fire glowing low and orange in the hearth. Enough light for me to see the fear on his face.

'What was that?'

'A gunshot,' he whispered. 'Come on, get up.'

I jumped out of bed, helping Lucas stand. If that was a gunshot, what did that mean? If that was Doug shooting, then what the hell was he shooting at? If it was Coates, where could we possibly go? I wanted to ask Lucas what he thought, but he was already heading toward the glass sliding door and tugging me with him.

The bitter sea air rushed in. I was only wearing my underpants and an old T-shirt Doug had given me. Lucas was wearing less, his chest completely bare. We couldn't go out there dressed like this. I yanked on his hand but he persisted, pulling me outside onto the veranda. The wind was strong and collected the shirt, whipping it up to expose my belly. I shivered and followed Lucas down the steps lightly coated with rain.

A dark shape rushed at us.

Coates!

He waved a gun as he shouted, but I couldn't hear him over the wind. Lucas immediately pushed me behind him, shielding me. But Coates was faster, herding us back up the steps and inside. Lucas stumbled through the door, his legs shaking.

'Sore leg, pretty boy?' Coates spat.

'Fuck you,' Lucas hissed back.

Coates kicked at him, his boot striking Lucas in the knee. He screamed, dropping to the carpet. Coates kicked him again. Lucas was face-down on the carpet, screaming, his body contorted. I stood frozen, the horror playing out in front of me. Silently, uselessly, I pleaded for some kind of intervention – something or someone to stop this from happening.

'Can you get a chair, please?'

I focused on the gun in his hand. It was a small black thing, much smaller than I thought a gun would be.

'Amanda, can you get a chair, please?' Coates repeated.

Lucas had stopped screaming and was sprawled on the

carpet, his mouth gaping. His breathing ragged, laboured.

I carried one of the kitchen chairs over, and placed it beside the bed as Coates directed.

'Can you take Lucas to the chair, please?'

I did as I was asked. I couldn't think to do anything else. Lucas managed to stand on one leg, head drooping, while I helped him into the chair.

'Now, reach into my pocket, please.'

I stared at him. For the first time I noticed that his nose was misshapen, swollen. His skin was tinged purple on one cheek. Injuries from his fight with Lucas? My breath faltered.

'The back pocket here. Now. Please.'

His back jeans pocket was bulging. Hand shaking, I pulled out a roll of duct tape. The same kind he'd used with Richards in the house.

'I want you to do as I say, now. Don't try anything. I want you to tape his wrists together behind the chair. Do it now.'

Crouching behind Lucas, I ripped the tape free, and wound some around his wrists. Coates stood next to me, watching. I entertained the thought of taping him loosely, so he could escape, but Coates was too close. Besides, I had the gut-churning feeling that Lucas wasn't going anywhere anytime soon.

'Now do each ankle please, to the chair leg on each side.'

Again, I did as asked. Silently, I implored Lucas to help me, to give me some idea, some indication as to what I should do. But his head hung forward, his face hidden behind his hair. He was silent. I was on my own. Tasting the metallic tang of blood, I released my lip from between my teeth.

'Now tape him around the middle, please. To the chair.'

I wound more tape around his naked belly, biting off the edge and sealing him against the chair. I nudged Lucas in the ribs as I did so, begging him to look at me. As I was about to move away, he lifted his head, and our eyes met. Then he looked up at Coates.

'Where's Doug?'

Doug! The gunshot!

'The old man can't help you.' Coates pointed the gun at me. 'Amanda, tape his mouth, please.'

'What did you do to him?' Lucas tried to move, but the tape held him fast. He tried again, the expression of pain stark. He lunged forward, legs bent, the chair still taped beneath him. Shouting, Coates pushed him back then punched Lucas in the jaw.

'Amanda,' Coates barked.

I was shaking hard. 'Did you shoot him?' I whispered.

'You don't ask the questions. Now, do as I say.'

'Why would you involve Doug?' I persisted. 'He didn't do anything.'

'You're here, aren't you?' He glared at me. 'You involved him by coming here.'

'How did you find us?' Lucas asked, his voice a low murmur. His lip had split back open, and blood was dripping off his chin.

Coates snorted. 'You think I couldn't figure it out? I knew you'd come running back here sooner or later, just like after the accident. Back to the old man who doesn't have a badge anymore, so he can't fucking save you!' He shouted the last words, spit flying.

Involuntarily, I took a step backwards.

'Amanda,' he snapped. 'Tape his fucking mouth shut, and do it now.'

My hands were wet, but I managed to rip off a piece of tape. Kneeling in front of Lucas, I stuck it over his mouth. I kissed each cheek, cradling his face, and knowing Coates was watching, pressed my mouth against his ear. 'I'll get us out of here, I promise.'

Jerked back, pain flared in my scalp.

I staggered backwards as Coates tugged on my hair again. Before I knew it, he'd pinned me face-first on the bed.

Muffled shouting from Lucas behind me.

Coates pressed his body against my back.

My cheek was squashed against the mattress, and he yanked my hair until my eyes watered. I tried to look behind me, but I was held firm. He bounced my head against the bed, and then I felt his breath on my ear, his beard scratching my skin.

'Do what I say and it will be better for you. No games.'

The pressure lifted, but I felt his hands on my hips, sliding down my bare legs. Panic rose in my throat and I could hear Lucas struggling and grunting through the tape. Coates gripped my legs and tugged me backwards. With a scream, I flung my arms forward, grasping for the sheets, but he was too fast, and my hands found nothing but air. My hips bumped up against his. *No! Not this. Please.*

I was hauled to my feet, dizzy. He shoved me towards Lucas, and I stumbled to him. His eyes were wide and frantic, sweat dripping down his temples, plastering his hair to his face. My throat closed. *This is it.* And the old cliché was right, my life was flashing before my eyes.

'Sit,' Coates ordered, using the gun to point at Lucas.

I crawled onto his lap, wrapping my bare legs around the chair so I could hold him tight.

My mind collected memories.

Marianne stirring sauce in the Alberto's kitchen.

Coates stood behind my right shoulder, the gun hovering near my head.

Teaching Oscar to ride a bike. Christmas at Mum and Dad's with boozy eggnog.

The gun pressed into my temple. The metal was cold. Lucas tucked his head against my chest. Sobs wracked his body.

Giovanni announcing Luisa's pregnancy. Champagne and dancing. Lucas smiling from behind the bar.

Lucas had his eyes closed, but I wanted him to look at me. He couldn't talk to me, he couldn't touch me. If I couldn't hear his voice one more time, or feel his hands, I at least needed him to look at me.

Dr Kim and his mugs of coffee. Marco sliding a diamond ring on my finger. Marco. Finally I could see his face clearly, and I didn't hate him anymore, not one little bit. My heart ballooned with love, gratitude and fear. A tremor climbed my spine, shaking my bones as I waited for the gunshot. As I waited for the end.

'Please,' I whispered. 'Can you take the tape off so we can say goodbye?'

'No,' Coates snapped, looming beside me. 'You can't say goodbye. I didn't get to say goodbye.'

My teeth were chattering, my body ice cold. I pressed my hands into the back of Lucas's head. His tears ran underneath the neck of my T shirt. The metal of the gun had warmed against my temple.

'Let Lucas apologise.'

The pressure lifted from my head, and Coates shook the gun at me. 'What?'

My heart was climbing in my throat. 'Let him say sorry for what he did to you and Julie,' I said. My voice shook, but hope reared its head when I noticed Coates clench his teeth. I loosened my grip on Lucas, slowly lowering my legs to the floor.

Coates was shaking his head, and the gun began to tremble in his hand. 'Don't you say her name ... Don't ...'

Lucas quieted. Finally he met my eyes, and the message in them was clear. *Run.*

I sprang to my feet.

Coates jolted forward, reaching out for me as I dashed past him. I found myself in the kitchen, spinning in a circle as Coates appeared in front of me.

'Nowhere to go,' he said, his teeth still clenched.

I shook so hard I could barely keep my feet. I gripped the kitchen bench, my mind racing but without one clear, distinct thought. There was no answer, no way out of this.

'I told you, no games. Will you come with me now, please?'

'I don't want to die.' I backed away from him, towards the kitchen sink. A knife on the cutting board. Apple seeds stuck to its blade, the cores brown and soggy. I shook my head; a knife was no match for a gun, but I couldn't just let Coates kill me. I didn't want to die.

'Please, come now.' He was holding out his hand to me, as if he was asking me to dance. Without thinking, I went to him. The adrenaline surged. I could not control my thoughts or my actions, or anything. I had no plan.

Coates held me against his chest, almost tenderly. 'I'm

sorry,' he whispered, and his beard scratched against my ear lobe. I cringed. His clothes were damp from the rain, or sweat. His heart thumped under his shirt. Was he nervous? He appeared cold and calm most of the time, but he certainly wasn't a career criminal. He'd had chances to end this earlier, before we wound up here at Doug's. And he hadn't. He'd gone from cool and distant to frantic and emotional, so maybe he couldn't actually bring himself to kill anyone. I had to hope so.

I lifted my head. His eyes were wide, wild, and shadowed underneath. So, he hadn't been sleeping then. He'd been hiding and running just as we had, and he'd found us. I wanted to know where he'd been before he'd figured it out.

I wanted to know how frightened he'd been.

He hooked a finger around a lock of my hair and tucked it behind an ear. 'You can say goodbye to him, if you behave for me.' His voice was a soft crackle. I frowned at him, and his lips lifted in an apologetic smile. 'If you promise not to run again, I'll let you say goodbye to him. None of this is your fault, so I can give you that.'

'How kind of you,' I murmured, then wished I hadn't. His eyes hardened, and the gun pushed into my lower back. Any moment a bullet could tear into my spine, but I didn't try and pull away. I searched for something to say that might possibly get through to him. 'I wish I'd known you before,' I said.

'Yeah?' He raised his eyebrows, but pressed the gun against me a little harder.

'Before the accident, I mean. Maybe you were a good guy before, someone worth knowing. You know, not a murderer.'

'I'm not the only murderer in the room.'

'Oh, that's right.' Anger rose, replacing the terror. *I've had enough of this shit.* 'It wasn't just a car accident. Lucas *murdered* Julie, didn't he?'

He blinked hard. 'Stop it.'

'Tell me, what was she like?' I pressed. 'What would she think about what you're doing now?'

Shaking his head, he widened his eyes. 'Don't try to fuck with me.'

'Never,' I whispered back. I lifted my knee and drove it into his balls as hard as I could. In the split second that he dropped to a crouch, I'd jumped out of his reach. Heart pounding, I turned towards Lucas when a sound tore through the tiny room with such ferocity it took me a moment to realise Coates had fired the gun.

I was on the ground.

Am I shot?

I couldn't feel anything, just the rush of adrenaline that pushed me across the kitchen floor with that shrill wail in my ears, my head, everywhere. I crawled towards the sink and with what felt like painful slowness, snaked my hand up towards the bench top, groping blindly until I found the handle of the knife. I pulled it down to me, tucking it under my body as Coates came up behind me. He grabbed me, flipped me over to face him. He straddled me, pinned my legs, the edge of the blade biting into the underside of my thigh. The barrel of the gun was inches from my face. He panted, his skin shining.

'Get up, get up! Get the fuck up!' he shouted, with such brutality it cut through the ringing in my ears. *I can't get up, you fucker.*

He gripped my throat with his free hand, squeezing hard.

My airway narrowed. My vision blurred. My world fell silent. He pushed his body weight forward – one hand choking me, the other holding the gun. His sweat dripped onto my face. His teeth were clenched.

His body wasn't protected.

Last chance.

Scrabbling for the knife, I tore it free from underneath me and swung my arm into his side. The blade connected.

Coates sat back. His hand unravelled from my neck. His mouth opened.

I jammed my fist forward as hard as I could. The knife plunged into his stomach and hot blood spilled over my fingers.

I drove the blade into him again.

The gun dropped like a lead weight onto my chest. I sucked in air as Coates dipped to the side, his face contorted. Filling my lungs, I rolled with him, wrenching the blade free.

I stabbed him again.

Again.

Again.

The handle became slippery with his blood and I couldn't grip it anymore. Coates slid to the linoleum floor, his legs still twisted over me. I shoved him away, grabbing the gun, and the knife, and edging away from him. His eyes were open wide, but the anger was gone.

Everything was gone.

Blood pooled underneath him, spreading out at the base of the kitchen cupboards. I gasped for air, my eyes streaming as I coughed and spluttered.

Lucas.

I tried to stand, but my legs wouldn't obey. So I crawled,

one weapon in each fist, leaving red prints as I went. A noise was grinding out of my throat. Not quite a groan, or a scream ... it was something else, something raw and animalistic, something I couldn't control.

Past the low fire I crawled, the shadowy figure of Lucas still tied to the chair my only focus. Frantically I tugged at the tape, but my fingers slid, bloody and useless, all over it. I wiped my hands against my bare legs, leaving trails of red behind, and eventually managed to unwind the tape. Lucas fell into me and we grabbed at each other, holding tight.

I was a mess of tears, or he was. I couldn't tell. Freeing his hands, we wiped at each other's faces, rocking back and forth, and the weight of what I'd done descended. There was a dead man in the kitchen. But it had to be him, not us. He'd come to Doug's to take our lives. But I'd ended it. It was finally over.

'Doug,' I gasped, rising to my knees. A gunshot had woken us, and Coates had said Doug couldn't help us. I clambered to my feet, wobbling over to the armchair. I slipped on my jacket. Lucas was silent; the darkness in his face, the weight of his loss, made my heart hammer against my ribs.

I ran out into the bracing wind, the icy drizzle. I leapt from the veranda, my bare feet slapping against the grassy track as I pelted up towards the house. Somehow, on such a dark night, the moon was out, full and white and beautiful. I followed it, the path leading under the shadowy eaves of Doug's house, around the peeling weatherboard and onto the veranda. The front door stood open, the wind tunnelling through it into the dim lounge room. The fire was out, smoke hissing from dark coals. I scanned the room as I thundered through it and into the kitchen.

'Doug,' I screamed.

The only light leaked out from the range hood over the stove. I flicked on the nearest switch I could find. How could it be so quiet? My breath rasped so loud it could peel off the wallpaper. I stopped then, in the centre of the kitchen, realising that for all I knew, there could be another Constable Richards in this house, someone else Coates had paid off to help him. I was here alone, without a weapon. But I had to find Doug. I couldn't stop now.

'Doug!'

I ran through the room, pausing in the door to the hallway. There he was. Crumpled on the floor against the wall, the phone receiver clutched in one fist, the cord twisted around his arm. I fumbled along the wall until my fingers bumped the switch, then I flicked it on. His head was down, his skin pasty white. Bessie lay curled up in his lap, her chin resting on his leg. I dropped to the floor next to them. A patch of blood covered Doug's chest. Biting my lip, I lifted his clammy face in my hands. A dribble of blood ran from the corner of his mouth, tracing a line over my wrist. But his eyes ... heavy-lidded, they latched onto mine.

'Doug.' I choked on a sob, pressing my forehead against his. I could hear the hum of dial tone from the receiver, and I reached for it.

'Police,' he whispered. 'I rang the police.'

'Okay.' I shook my head, not knowing what to do. In the movies, they pressed on gunshot wounds to stop the bleeding, didn't they? Across the hall, I whisked a crocheted blanket off Doug's bed and wrapped it around him. He was murmuring something, blood bubbling between his lips. I leaned in closer.

'Luke.'

I bit my lip as the tears spilled out. 'He's okay,' I managed, before burying my face into his shoulder. I killed Coates, I wanted to say. I left Lucas alone down there, with Coates dead on the floor. Instead, I clutched Doug and Bessie to me and sobbed.

Chapter 16

The red and blue lights cut through the curtains. When the group of officers rushed into the house, weapons drawn, I barely flinched. A heavily-moustached man peeled me away from Doug and Bessie and I gave in, leaning back against the wall, my pale legs streaked with blood. They were stiff and uncooperative. The officer examined me as I sat there in my underpants, while the rest of them swarmed around Doug. The police officer lifted my chin, his eyes narrowed. 'Are you hurt?'

I tried to swallow, but my mouth was too dry. I didn't know how long I'd waited with Doug in the hallway. The concept of time and reality had been lost.

'Are you hurt?' Officer Moustache asked again.

'I killed him.'

He bristled. 'Graham Coates?'

I nodded and hung my head. I needed to see Lucas, to make sure he was okay. I couldn't believe I'd left him alone down there, but I didn't have a choice. All my careful planning and reasoning I'd practiced in the past suddenly didn't exist anymore. It was primitive; what I'd done tonight was something I never thought I'd have to do. Ever. But I hadn't hesitated. I'd slammed that knife into him with such ferocity … I had lost myself in that moment.

They moved Doug slowly out of the hallway while Bessie whined, searching for an answer in my face. I held her in my lap and closed my eyes. The murmur of voices carried through from the kitchen. A cool hand touched my knee. A female paramedic crouched in front of me.

'Amanda,' she said gently. Her voice was as smooth as honey. Her red hair was tied tightly in a bun, and her cheeks were smooth, porcelain white. I blinked at her. 'Can you stand up for me?'

She led me out of the house and onto the cold front veranda. Flashing lights everywhere. Two police cars, two ambulances. Doug was in the back of one, his big belly pointing upwards from the stretcher. The paramedic wrapped a scratchy blanket around me, and indicated for me to sit. I sat on the same wooden chair where I'd called Marianne the first night here. With Bess heavy on my bare feet, I went through the same routine I'd gone through the night at my place. I followed the torch beam from side to side. I took deep breaths when she asked. She poked at me under the flashlight, asking me questions. I had my own question, but I had to pry my lips apart to ask it.

'Where's Lucas?'

She guided me from the chair to the closest police car. I crawled into the back seat, Bess jumping in after me. 'He'll be right behind us.'

*

I sat on a plastic seat in a long white corridor. To my right, a set of doors were closed and looming ominously – SURGICAL. A nurse occupied the seat next to me, her voice the only sound in the silence. She was talking about her cat; it had been dropping mice on her doormat lately.

Finally I was back in the city, but this place was alien, uncomfortable. The smell of antiseptic set my sinuses on fire. It covered the smell of the ill, but it didn't block the sight of them. I saw them everywhere in their robes, with their IVs, groaning in their beds. I wanted to run and run until I reached my apartment, where I could settle back into the familiar, surrounded by my belongings. But I knew I couldn't do that. I had to wait – for Lucas, for Marianne, for Cam, for the police. I hadn't seen anyone yet.

I cradled my hand in my lap. It was heavily bandaged to the size of a boxing glove – cumbersome, awkward, and hot with pain. I hadn't even known it was cut open until afterwards, when a nurse had explained that my hand would have been slipping off the bloody knife handle and on to the blade. She'd cleaned me up, filling me with antibiotics. But I wondered if it was too late. Was his blood inside of me? Had it worked its way into my wounds? Would it be inside me forever?

I heard a rattling sound and sat straighter in the chair. The nurse's voice fell quiet and I stared past her to the end of the corridor. A bed was wheeled into view, coming around the corner and heading towards us. The nurse gave me a gentle nudge and I stood, walking over. A male nurse in blue scrubs smiled at me. I looked down, and there he was.

Wrapped in a white blanket, his hair tucked under a cap, his eyes half-open and glassy.

'Can he hear me?' I asked the nurse.

He nodded. 'We've given him a sedative. But he's awake.'

I leaned over the bars on the side of the bed. 'Lucas?'

His head swivelled towards me, eyes widening. 'Amanda.'

I pressed my unbandaged hand into his. He was wearing a paper band around his wrist. I squeezed his fingers gently, but he didn't squeeze back. He was drifting, his eyes closing. He murmured my name again before sleep claimed him.

*

I sat by the window in a vinyl armchair, waiting. I was told his surgery would take a few hours, and I was watching the tick of the clock. Two other women shared the room, older women, who seemed to find me fascinating. They must have been wondering what I was doing here. I was too.

Only an hour had passed when I heard a commotion in the corridor.

'Yes, I am bringing in food, for God's sake. It's chicken, okay? Just chicken.'

I shot out of my chair and shouted her name.

Marianne barrelled through the door, a covered casserole dish in her hands. Porcelain clattered as she thumped it down on the bedside table and then her arms were around me, squeezing tight. I buried my face in her hair, inhaling her familiarity, the smell of Alberto's. She wasn't saying anything, and when she finally let me go, her cheeks were wet with tears.

'They wouldn't let me call you,' I said, my own eyes filling.

She shook her head. 'It's okay, I know everything. The police came.' She shook her head again. 'I know everything.' She grabbed me, rocking me in her arms.

The two patients watched us, plainly mesmerised. We sat on the edge of my bed, and she lifted the lid of the dish to show me the roasted garlic chicken inside. I laughed.

'You're an idiot. I've missed you.'

She swallowed hard. 'Cam has Bessie, okay? He picked her up.'

'Good. They haven't talked to me yet. The police.'

'They will. They're coming today. But then you can go home.'

Relief washed over me almost violently. I knew that when Marianne came she'd be armed with information.

'So I'm not going to prison?'

'No, of course not. It was self-defence. You did nothing wrong.'

'I don't know if that's true.'

'Trust the police.' Her voice had hardened. 'They'll look after you. It'll be okay.'

'Tell me what you know,' I whispered.

Her face was pale, a bit too pale, but she nodded. 'Doug's okay. He'll be in hospital for a while, though. Lucas is going to be fine. And ...' She grabbed my hand. 'The rest is over. You stabbed him nine times.'

'No,' I breathed. I bit my lip. *Nine times.* 'No ...'

She held my eyes. 'It's over now,' she repeated. 'They've got Richards, and the rest is over. You can go home, back to normal.'

I tried to laugh. 'Back to normal ...'

*

A cool hand to my forehead woke me. I blinked until my mother's face came into focus. She looked awful with makeup caked in the creases around her eyes and mouth, hair windblown.

'Mum?'

She seemed to flinch when she heard my voice, taking half a step away from the bed. She smiled a shaky smile. 'Amanda ... honey ...'

I struggled to prop myself into a sitting position, and when I did, I noticed Dad hovering by the doorway.

'Dad.'

'How are you feeling, love?' He came closer, and I didn't miss the gentle prod between Mum's shoulder blades.

'I'm okay, it's just my hand.' I held it up for them to see. 'I'm waiting for Lucas to get out of surgery.'

'Marianne called us,' Mum started. She took a breath, averting her eyes as she did so. 'She really cares about you. She's like a sister to you, always there ... isn't she?'

I reached for a cup of water on the bedside table, taking my time to reply. 'Yes, she is.'

'And this ... Lucas, is he going to be all right?'

I stared at her. She was trying hard, but she looked so uncomfortable, so out of place. When I'd woken with her hand stroking my head, I'd believed she was doing what a mother should do; comforting me, telling me that everything was going to be all right no matter what.

'Yes, he'll be all right.'

'Good,' she nodded. She glanced pleadingly at my dad.

'Is there anything we can do for you?' Dad asked, perching

next to me on the mattress. 'Would you like to come home with us for a while, to recover?'

'That's okay. Thanks. Marianne's going to stay with me.'

'Well, that's nice,' Mum piped up. 'With one hand all bandaged up like that it'll be hard to cook for yourself, won't it?' She smoothed her hair, shifting from foot to foot. 'And she'll make sure you're safe, so you won't be there all alone. That's great.'

'Yeah,' I sighed. 'My apartment isn't very secure.' I bit my lip. 'You know, I'm pretty tired, so ...'

'Oh!' Mum said brightly; too brightly. 'Yes, we'll let you rest.'

'You call us if you need anything,' Dad whispered, kissing my cheek. 'We're only a phone call away.'

Mum leaned over to kiss my forehead, and I closed my eyes, choosing not to watch them leave.

*

Marianne's car screeched to a halt alongside the kerb. Lucas and Cam's house was exactly as I remembered it, box-like and ugly. But unlike the day I'd come to ask Lucas who Graham Coates was, it didn't look cold and lifeless, and I wasn't filled with dread.

Cam was waiting for us in the driveway, beer bottle in his fist. Bessie sat patiently at his feet, wagging her tail. He hugged me tightly, leading me towards the house. Marianne followed behind, her arms full of shopping bags.

Inside the lounge room music murmured, voices barely audible beneath it. Everyone stopped and stared when I walked in. Giovanni looked exhausted, his eyes shadowed.

Luisa clapped her hand over Oscar's shoulder, who didn't run at me. It was like a wake. It was miserable.

'What kind of welcome home is this?' I asked, trying to smile.

Luisa nudged Oscar, who bolted into my arms. I lifted him up, ignoring the throb under the bandage. He pressed his mouth against my ear. 'Are you better now?' he whispered.

'Yes,' I whispered back.

'Lucas looks sick.'

'He's almost better too. He'll be okay.'

He moved his small face in front of mine, grinning. 'Cam said I can help make the barbecue.'

I smiled back. 'That sounds like fun.'

*

Cam showed me to Lucas's bedroom. I opened the door and peered inside. Lucas rested on top of a grey striped doona. Pale-faced, eyes shut, he wore baggy pants and a tatty T shirt.

I hadn't seen his room before, and took a minute to take it in. A tall chest of drawers with the remnants of stickers peeling from the pine veneer stood against the opposite wall, boxer shorts spilling from one of the drawers at the top. On the walls hung a few of his mother's paintings, including another portrait of Doug's house at the beach. A pair of scuffed black Docs sat on the carpet beside a pair of rubber thongs and a battered pair of Cons. A surfboard dominated a corner, its point hidden under a jacket that had been hung there. On his bedside table, a pile of books had gathered dust.

I tiptoed over to the bed and sank to the carpet beside him. I hesitated to wake him, even though he'd told me to. Sucking in a big breath, I reached for his hand.

'Hey,' I whispered.

Opening his eyes, he smiled, thin-lipped. 'You took your time.'

I laughed. 'Oh, really? Sorry. It's hard to dress myself with this.' I held up my bandaged hand and he frowned.

'I'd love to help dress you.'

'I think you should focus on getting yourself better.'

'I'll be right.'

I squeezed his hand. 'Promise?'

He lifted a shoulder. 'Sure, I've done it all before.' He grunted as he tried to sit himself up and immediately I pushed him back down.

'You're supposed to stay in bed.'

'I need you to come closer,' he murmured.

I rested my head on his chest, listening to the thump of his heart, his slow sigh. 'We'll visit Doug when you're a bit better,' I whispered. 'I'm sure he misses Bessie.'

'Okay,' he answered, his voice cracking. 'You'll come with me?'

I curled my arm across his belly, gently, trying to protect us both from pain. I soaked in the warmth from his skin, my eyes drifting closed. 'Of course I will.'

Acknowledgements

I'd like to thank everyone who supported me during the writing of this book. It means so much.

Firstly, a big thank you to my editor, Amanda, for being so patient and ultimately making this book much better.

Thank you to Kerry and Aderyn, for giving your time generously and answering all my questions.

Louis, thanks for the amazing cover. It's perfect.

Thank you to FF and Barbara, for teaching me so much about writing. And CJ, thanks for your support too.

Mum and Dad, I can't thank you enough for encouraging me. Lois and Andrew, Adam, Joel, Aaron, and my whole extended family – you're great. Thanks for being there.

And lastly, thank you Ashley, for pushing me to do better and for loving me no matter what.

About Brooke

Brooke Linford is an Australian writer and editor. She lives in Victoria with her partner, where she visits the beach as often as possible.

Broken is her first novel.

If you enjoyed this book please consider leaving a review. Thanks!